"OLD SCORES
illustrates why Delbanco
deserves a wider following....

A lovely, sad tale of love and loss, which few authors may spin with as much conviction as Nicholas Delbanco.... The people inhabiting his novels are life-sized, no larger than that; and their emotions are true.... Delbanco remains a treasure."

—Ft. Worth Star-Telegram

"Love is deeper than flesh. It is the imprint one person makes on another, and in the sure hands of Nicholas Delbanco, OLD SCORES is a lovely and honest telling of how that imprint endures."

—Washington Post Book World

"[Nicholas Delbanco] wrestles with the abundance of his gifts as a novelist the way other men wrestle with their deficiencies."

—John Updike

"A sad, convincing, autumnal tale of love lost, found, and lost again, by old pro Delbanco.... Delbanco narrates his lovers' plight in a spare, emotionally exact tone, and his characters have the complexity and fragility of real life.... A moving exploration of a believably passionate love, and of its subtle, powerful, persistent impact on the lives of two stubborn romantics."

—Kirkus Reviews

more...

"This spare, haunting evocation of enduring love brings new life to one of our great old romances. Salvaging love from the ruins, Delbanco's modern-day Abelard and Heloise are full of heat and heart and extraordinarily moving."
—Andrea Barrett, winner of the National Book Award and author of *Ship Fever*

"For all this novel achieves—a subtle postmortem of the 60s; a good stiff scouring of liberal education's hollow idyll of redemption; a canny send-up of my own beleaguered generation—OLD SCORES is at its considerable best, a simple and delicate love story. It's nice to see a real writer—and a man, no less—writing such a book as this. I read it in a sitting."
—Richard Ford, author of *Independence Day*

"Delbanco gives us here an Abelard and Heloise for our time, and if his comparison, of necessity, at first diminishes, it also enlarges; Paul and Elizabeth are legitimate heirs.... We may characterize his writing at every point in this complex and difficult enterprise by its acute intelligence, by its compassion."
—*Review of Contemporary Fiction*

"Nicholas Delbanco has had a distinguished career, both as a teacher and writer.... The novel is poignant, echoing some of Delbanco's best work."
—*Detroit Free Press*

ALSO BY
NICHOLAS DELBANCO

Fiction
In the Name of Mercy
The Writers' Trade, & Other Stories
About My Table, & Other Stories
Stillness
Sherbrookes
Possession
Small Rain
Fathering
In the Middle Distance
News
Consider Sappho Burning
Grasse 3/23/66
The Martlet's Tale

Non-Fiction
Running in Place: Scenes from the South of France
The Beaux Arts Trio: a Portrait
Group Portrait: Conrad, Crane, Ford, James, & Wells

Books Edited

Talking Horse: Bernard Malamud on Life and Work (w. A. Cheuse)
Speaking of Writing: Selected Hopwood Lectures
Writers and Their Craft; Short Stories & Essays on the Narrative
(w. L. Goldstein)
Stillness and Shadows (two novels by John Gardner)

OLD
SCORES

NICHOLAS
DELBANCO

WARNER BOOKS

A Time Warner Company

Copyright © 1997 by Nicholas Delbanco
All rights reserved.

Warner Books, Inc., 1271 Avenue of the Americas,
New York, NY 10020

Visit our Web site at www.twbookmark.com

 A Time Warner Company

Originally printed in hardcover by Warner Books, Inc.
First Trade Printing: November 2000
10 9 8 7 6 5 4 3 2 1

The Library of Congress has cataloged the hardcover edition as follows:

Delbanco, Nicholas.
Old scores / Nicholas Delbanco.
p. cm.
ISBN 0-446-52046-2
ISBN 0-446-67450-8 (pbk.)
I. Title
PS3554.E442043   1997
813'.54—dc21   97-6254
                                              CIP

Book design by Giorgetta Bell McRee
Cover design by Honi Werner

Elena

Où est la très sage Hellois
Pour qui fut chastré, puis moine
Pierre Esbaillart à Saint-Denis?
Pour son amour eut cette essoyne . . .
    Mais où sont les neiges d'antan?

François Villon
Ballade des Dames du Temps Jadis

OLD
SCORES

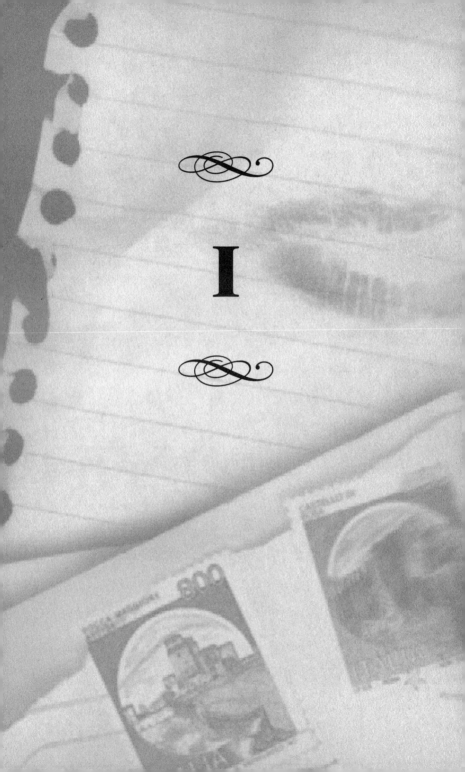

I

HE WAS A clever man. That much was obvious. Those who watched him in his infancy would claim it had been obvious to anyone who knew Paul Ballard from the start. Twelve months old, he learned the alphabet and enjoyed conducting while the radio played Bach. Bach was his father's favorite, but his mother's tastes were catholic, and she liked everything, she liked to say, from Frank Sinatra to Billie Holiday to Gabriel Fauré. It didn't matter, really, what music they were playing as long as music played.

Little Paul seemed to agree. He would raise his arms up from the carriage or high-chair and wave his hands delightedly when he heard Mozart or Bloch. He imitated the difference between *adagio* and *vivace* and also soft and loud. Paul did so in the fashion of an orchestra conductor, expansive and imperious, and often on the beat. He hummed while eating oatmeal or sucking on anything sweet, and when he sang Happy Birthday he did so, always, in tune. He'll be a musician, his grandmother said, and his mother said, Oh I don't know, maybe what he wants to be is a policeman. Maybe he's directing traffic, not an orchestra. You mark my words, his grandmother repeated, there's harmony in the child's soul . . .

He liked to play checkers, then chess. He taught himself arithmetic at three. He enjoyed the back-and-forth of *This little piggy* or *Old MacDonald*, and he knew every single answer to the question of what noises were produced by horse or dog or lamb or owl or cow. *Oink-oink* he answered when asked about pigs, and *meeow meeow* about cats. He memorized his multiplication tables, seven times seven and nine times twelve and, later, he could manage complicated fractions and do long division in his head. He was an intelligent boy. Everybody said so, and some of them were envious, and when he won the spelling bee there were many who called him too big for his britches, too stuck-up for his own good.

"Metempsychosis" was the word; he knew it in fourth grade. The class divided into half, not by size places but the alphabet, and his team routinely won. They lined up along the blackboard, and the teacher would read out a word on a card—"euchre," say, or "palimpsest" or perhaps "vastation." If you spelled it right the other team would get a new word for their turn, but if you spelled it wrong the other team would have a chance to get it right. Paul knew this was unfair.

(Later, he explained it all to Robert Askeles. If you spelled "euchre" with a terminal "er," or thought it meant the eucharist and were disqualified, then your opponent could avoid at least one way to lose and therefore had a better chance to win.

"That's life," said Robert Askeles. "That's how it works in the world."

"What world? The world of spelling bees?"

"Correct."

"Why do we call them 'bees,' I wonder. Because we buzz and hum?"

"Correct. We *drone*."

"Abecedarian," said Paul. "That's the word for a person who barely can read. First 'a,' then 'b,' then 'c.'"

"I thought it was 'analphabetic.'"

"No.")

Language was his strong suit, and had been all along. In fourth grade, when he was ten years old, a perfect consonance obtained between what he heard, saw, and wrote. The word "consonance," for instance, might end with a final "ts" and mean something altogether different; so might the word "instance" itself. But never for an instant did young Ballard get it wrong, and he failed to understand how other boys or even Robert Askeles could not *see* language spoken, as though the letters and the syllables inscribed upon the teacher's prompt cards were etched upon the *luminous* and *circumambient* air. When the atmosphere was sufficiently cold and he could watch his own breath steam, it was as though the alphabet became *corporeal* if *evanescent,* and all these words were words he knew by seventh grade.

Then he learned languages. When they started him on Latin it was as though, from some previous existence, he already comprehended it; so too with French and Spanish, those exfoliating leaves upon the twig of the one branch, those roots of a multiform tree. *Comprende? Tu comprends?* He did not need to study them or scrutinize their grammars; they made musical arrangements like the ones he could hear in his head. Or, to change the figure, it was as though a line might complete and thereafter compound itself into echo and silence: half-remembered, foreordained.

"Clever, clever," said his teachers. *"Ja, ja, precisely, gewiss."*

Nor did German prove intractable, though he took small pleasure in its utterance and preferred the elisions of Danish and Dutch. Through grade school and high school and college and graduate school Ballard stood at the head of his class. Yet those who watched him whispered, and some were dismissive or scornful: if he's so smart, they asked, how come he isn't rich? *Smarty-pants,* they called him, *smart-aleck* and *smart-ass.*

There came a time when language ceased to interest him, when the articulation of sweet sounds together no longer seemed the point. It was as though the mind's refrain (a snatch of song, a whistled chorus or repeated modulation) were code he might learn how to crack. Now what he chose to study stretched beyond the reach of syntax—that field where music, common parlance, and notation intersect. With no conscious application Ballard scanned it while he tried to sleep, or heard it in the shower: tonic and dominant, octave and chord . . .

(Later he discussed it all with Robert Askeles. If we postulate, for example, the answer that is "God," then what might be the question?

"Who said that? Gertrude Stein?"

"A variation on her theme. It's not, perhaps, original."

"What? Faith?"

"The nameless name. The dialectic."

Robert made a movement of impatience. "You're talking in riddles again."

"The question suggests less the *answer* than *asker*. Let's call it, for the sake of argument, our epistemological uncertainty . . ."

"God, Mr. Philosopher . . ."

"No.")

Here rhetoric applied. The tactics of debate club and the strategies of cross-examination were skills that served him well. Those teachers who took pleasure in having such a student helped secure for him an NEH Fellowship and a John Simon Guggenheim Memorial Fellowship and two separate stipends for research from the ACLS. He moved from job to job, from city to countryside searching for knowledge or what they called then—in the fashion of the period—enlightenment.

"We are professionals," he liked to say, "*professors*, if you will, but what do we *profess*?"

He worked at City College, then Cornell, where he established the beginnings of a widespread reputation. He married and divorced. His wife needed to be with a person, she said, who believed she was special and didn't make her feel like a fool simply for *wanting* to maximize her personality potential and for *deciding* to actualize herself and be self-actualized. Their marriage had been a mistake. They could correct it, she said. Her new lover was in politics; he owned a real-estate company and would be a state senator soon, and he makes me *happy*, Paul, he doesn't think I'm stupid or worthless and I want to have his child . . .

In 1966, on his thirty-second birthday, Ballard moved

to the small college town of Catamount, Vermont. At Catamount College he prospered, writing articles and books. There were those who flocked to study what he taught.

What she knew of him was just the usual sort of shit, an old man making eyes at her across a crowded room. Except it wasn't crowded: twelve disciples on the floor and chairs and couches, doing Kant. Charette had made a bet with her: if you wear your leather miniskirt and nothing underneath at all he'll lose his famous cool. Dawn tried it too; they had a bet, the three of them, to see which one—sitting in Ballard's logic class, sharing a couch—could get him to forget what he'd been saying, or cough, or maybe light his pipe. It was "The Categorical Imperative," that much she could remember, and he had been critiquing by way of introduction the Kantean assertion that pure reason could prevail. The dormitory living room he taught them in still smelled of last night's weed, and beer, and Monday morning was a bitch, and when she spread her legs he lit his pipe.

It was 1969. It was April 21, Elizabeth remembered, the snow on the crest of the mountains, melting, and that yellow haze around the willow trees that meant there would be spring. She never believed it, not really, but then the ice cracked up along the river and birds began to sing again and you could *feel* things thaw. She was a junior at Catamount College, and Locke and Wittgenstein and Kant were not exactly the hottest of topics and she had a sinus headache and a paper due that afternoon for "Mythopoesis and Literature" she'd not even started to write. So Professor blue-eyes Ballard could discuss his categorical imperative till everything got old, and cold, because the beauty and rigor of logic was escaping her this morning, because the milk in her coffee cup curdled, and if it wasn't for her friends on either side scratching away in their loose-leaf notebooks she might just fall asleep.

Outside, Beth watched the snow melt and the gutters drip. Sun made the meadow steam. There were two samplers on the wall, stitched by some local lady in red, white and blue. One read *Today Is the Beginning of the Rest of Your Life,* and one read *Home, Sweet Home.* There was also a black-and-white photograph of a boy in a top hat and sandwich board; the placard he was wearing warned *The End of the World Is at Hand.* Last night she had found herself joining a circle, her right hand in a stranger's left, her left hand in a stranger's right, in a dark barn chanting *Om* . . .

Dawn had a thing for their teacher and wondered if he knew. She wondered if he understood how sexy he looked in his blue jeans and tweeds, his brown hair curling at his collar and cheekbones to die for, his old leather vest. He was severe and brilliant and rugged and intense; he was everything Dawn wanted, and famous in their world. Once, she told Elizabeth, when he gave a party for a painter who was having a show at the college she excused herself and went upstairs in Ballard's house and took off all her clothes and pressed herself into his sheets. She wondered, could he tell?

He lived two miles north of campus, in a red farmhouse with an apple orchard, and one night the three girls got high in the orchard and crept in the dark to his library window. He sat there, reading, alone. They watched him in the easy-chair, smoking, making notes in the margin of the leather book he was holding, his personal copy of Alfred North Whitehead—and that was what, Beth confessed to him later, much later, she couldn't forget (the frown on his face, the purse-lipped concentration, the reading glasses that he wore and the way he licked the pencil stub and smoothed his hair back absently, focusing, mouthing what he'd no doubt offer up in class next day as an offhand perception, a clever demurral) and that was when she understood that he required pity (though maybe it was just the grass, the sweet night breeze and crescent moon and Dawn and Charette on either side, rapt, palpitant) and would be hard to dismiss.

Richard Nixon was getting her down. Her parents had voted for Nixon, of course, and so did everybody else in what they called their crowd. Received collective wisdom from the residents of Grosse Pointe Shores was that the Chicago Eight—Abbie Hoffman, Rennie Davis, Jerry Rubin and the rest—were clowns. It's a circus, her father announced.

What's so bad about a circus, she could remember asking, you used to take me to Ringling Brothers, Barnum & Bailey, and her mother said we're not joking here, Lizzie, all right? Some of these people are dangerous, with their weapons and clenched fists. That man Huey Newton's a crazy man, you can see it in the clothes he wears, and the other Black Panther, that man Eldridge Cleaver, is a convicted rapist, isn't he, so we can't blame the FBI for watching what they do. The problem with this country is that you kids are wrecking it, with your ridiculous slogans and your signs for Flower Power and Make Love, Not War.

She had reminded them of what they seemed to be in danger of forgetting: there's a Bill of Rights, remember? A right of free speech and assembly. Don't delude yourself, Lizzie, her father declared: it's what we used to call treason, and anyplace else but this country they'd shoot you or put you in jail.

Her mother sipped a second drink and, spearing the olive, agreed: You're giving aid and comfort to the enemy, darling, and Ho Chi Minh can applaud all your friends on TV. Anytime he feels like it he can read a transcript of the things your friends are saying and believe he'll win the war.

She had controlled herself and bit her tongue and swallowed her mother's chilled stilton and cream of asparagus soup. The chandelier was bright. It didn't matter how she told them Ho Chi Minh had better things to do than watch Americans wave banners on the nightly news, or how he wasn't reading Abbie Hoffman or admiring Jane Fonda but delivering North Vietnam out of historical bondage; he was George Washington and Simón Bolívar and Mao and maybe Jesus too all rolled up into one.

Then Katie came to clear and then she brought in the

roast. Her father carved. Elizabeth wanted to scream. You're part of the solution or you're a part of the problem, she tried to tell her parents, and tear-gas won't fix Amerika, or your precious CIA. The winds of change are everywhere, and it doesn't take a weatherman to know which way they blow . . .

While Katie brought the coffee, her father leaned back in his chair. It's a strange way to change, Mr. Sieverdsen said, if you really want to make a change why not give your trust fund away?

"Why not?" her mother echoed, "if it's what you *really* want . . ."

But this was just an empty threat, and all of the family knew it: she wasn't twenty-one years old and couldn't touch the principal till she turned twenty-five. What her grandfather had left for her—the not-inconsiderable resources, as the trust's executor expressed it, of a lifetime spent in service and, thereafter, speculation—would remain intact. So Beth went back to Catamount and wrote poetry and danced and studied the Western Rationalist Tradition and the History of Logic with Ballard while he smoked.

After class they walked to Commons; it was eleven o'clock. Did you notice how he looked at me, asked Dawn; when he loosened his tie and leaned back in the chair, did you see the way he stared? When you answered that question about population, the one about Malthus and life being brief, did you see him lick his lips?

The day was warming up. Beth did have a paper to write. There was a spider on the door and it was amazing, wasn't it, all winter you couldn't find insects and then the snow begins to melt and suddenly there're spiderwebs in every direction you look. If I close my eyes, she asked Dawn and Charette, how can you two convince me that it isn't night?

"We can tell you what the time is."

"Time? It's only a convention. A decision about where to draw time zones, a collective agreement reached by cartographers."

"We can determine if it's light outside."

"Light?"

"The sun on your skin. That bright sensation—sunlight, warmth."

"To a blind person the light would mean nothing."

"We can *pinch* you," said Charette, and suited her action to words.

Having grown up in Manhattan, Ballard delighted in southern Vermont. He enjoyed his vegetable garden and the smell of fresh-baked bread and liked to build a fire with his own orchard's wood. When a neighbor gave him syrup it was a pleasure to know the tapped tree, and to have carried the pail. The village of North Catamount conveyed the feel of rural life but none of its harsh exigency; the poverty he noticed was, when authentic, picturesque.

The *pittoresque*, in fact, engaged both Ballard's scholarly and philosophical attention. His experience of cities had given him, as he was fond of saying, a blank primed canvas for the country of the mind. The nearby Hudson River Valley provided him with just such landscapes; a vista not so much reported on as imagined and ideal. The painter Grandma Moses lived and worked not far from Catamount, and the scenes she had preserved in oil—however primitively rendered—were what Ballard too surveyed. He liked to drive past low white clapboard farmhouses and stone walls and stockponds and mills. The imaginary number *i* (a negative which, when multiplied by itself, remained a mirrored negative) became a kind of template for the text of place. What he wrote on now were buildings as containers; the apartment *complex* and monastic *simple* cell.

His colleagues were engaging and some of them of interest; his students had—one or two of them did, anyhow—real flair. When Beth Sieverdsen approached him outside Commons, holding a cup of snack bar coffee and a raisin bagel, he had been cleaning his pipe. His Balkan Sobranie was too damp to smoke; he was thinking of giving it up.

"Do you mind if I ask you a question?"

"Of course not, Beth."

"I wanted to ask you about it in class. I didn't get the chance to. It seemed so, oh, well, *personal* . . ."

"Go right ahead."

"Do you ever, I mean, find it difficult? To concentrate?"

"In class?"

"Whatever. It did seem that way, this morning—hard to concentrate, I mean. I mean, Professor, for *me.*"

He tamped his tobacco down, hard. At Catamount the teachers were unranked; there were no full or associate or assistant professors or instructors, and so when she called him "Professor" it was with mock respect.

"I always feel"—she raised her coffee cup—"when spring starts exploding around us like this, it's like the world is saying, okay, all right, just *notice* things. We'll give you all a second chance, a chance to *fix* things, right?"

"And what would you say needs fixing?" Ballard brought out a match. "What requires our correction?"

"Oh, everything. It's like we got it wrong before and now's our chance to start all over. With what you've been calling a *tabula rasa*: clean slate." She laughed. "I know that isn't what he meant, John Locke, I mean, but that's the way I feel about it on a great spring day like this one, a *great* spring day with all this stuff melting and growing, like the only thing that matters is to begin again. Like that pussy willow, for instance, or the crocus there . . ."

He studied her: the coltish legs, the long blond hair, the face that would be beautiful when settled into *gravitas*. A delivery truck—Baked Goods & Breads—pulled into the loading dock slowly, honking, and he made himself watch its arrival. On Commons Lawn two boys were playing catch.

"Last night," the girl continued, "I went to that performance in the Carriage Barn. I didn't see you there, I guess you didn't come. But it was really something at the end of *Dionysos*, when they cut the lights, it was like all of us were breathing in unison, chanting in unison, like we were part of one enormous body, and it didn't matter, really, what part belonged to whom. Like I could be your elbow, maybe, or *inside* your elbow, breathing it, and you could be my knee. What I mean is, oh, in class this morning it *still* felt that way; it did just a little bit, didn't it?"

He lit his pipe. His match flared and then guttered out. "You're referring to the mysteries."

"What mysteries?"

He puffed. "Eleusis. The Orphics and their devotees believed that we were all once one, a unity, but now we're the scattered components of a single whole . . ."

A golden retriever chased a Frisbee; a bluejay shrilled behind him, and half the school, it seemed, was lying on the lawn.

"So what worshipers must do," he explained, "is celebrate together and assemble their separate parts. Like Isis hunting Osiris, or the dismembered Dionysos Zagreus, or the whole process of transubstantiation when Catholics swallow the host. This notion of union, *com*-union, it isn't only Greek."

"I know," she said.

"Oh?"

"It's what I'm writing. Well, planning to write." She offered him a bite of raisin bagel. He refused. "It's the subject of my paper."

"On?"

"I'm doing *The Bacchae* for 'Myth and Lit.' That's why I've got this orgy stuff on my mind this morning, probably. All those instructions to *Take of my body. Eat, drink.* That, and the spiders."

"The spiders?"

"Remember when we talked about that cave in *The Symposium*? They're spinning, yes."

"I'm not sure I follow," said Ballard.

"They make me feel so naked."

And then she walked away.

So that was the beginning, and she had no idea at all where it was going to end. Spring settled in, and she was restless, and nothing she could do or say would make a bit of difference to President Nixon, or to Vice-President Agnew or Attorney General John Mitchell or H. R. "Bob" Haldeman, all those criminals in government who had tear-gas and the F.B.I. and shock troops on their side. More and more she hated Washington and what it represented and how she felt betrayed. More and more her friends were strangers, and she held herself in readiness for what would surely come: revolution, the leveling wind.

Dawn started seeing a senior from Amherst, the co-captain of their soccer team who planned to join a bank. Beth said, you can't be serious, but Dawn insisted it was serious, and when they came back one weekend from visiting his family in Connecticut she said they were engaged. They would marry in the fall. What about our

Mr. Wonderful, Beth asked, and Dawn said I'm resigning from the Fan Club; you can have him, he's all yours.

Charette was into celibacy; her parents were designers who had met on a charette—a team-executed all-night architecture project—which was how she got her name. She was throwing pots and plates and she believed the clay demanded absolute dedication, and it could tell when she had been distracted. The nature of her hands and wrists and everything they were involved in would reveal itself to clay. So for the month before her senior show she planned to eat and sleep in the ceramics studio and wouldn't even *shower* without the clay's permission since the soap and water rinsed her work away . . .

Blue-eyes Ballard was discussing liberty. In class he avoided her side of the room, focusing on air. He was saying there's a difference in our value system between liberty and autonomy, and he defined the terms and said let's distinguish between them. Let us begin, class, by considering the notion of *limits, limitation,* whether positive or negative. A romantic yearning for escape, as exemplified by Baudelaire's celebrated refrain, *N'importe où, hors de ce monde*—"Anywhere out of this world"—or in Coleridge's drug-induced vision of Kubla Kahn and Xanadu, the stately pleasure dome decreed: all such escapist fantasy, said Ballard, relies on circumscription and the idea of enclosure. As boundlessness requires the prior concept of location, so the very *subject* of escape is *predicated* on and organized by confinement. He lit his pipe, laboriously, as though needing to reflect on the distinction between independence and freedom and in order, he explained, to situate the terms in both a collective and personal context: would you say, he asked the window, that my liberty deprives you, in any degree, of your own? Am I permitted, for instance, to sit in your chair or eat your porridge or decide to lie down in your bed?

She waited for him after class. The sky outside darkened; the others had left.

"Why did you pick those examples?"

"Which ones?"

"From Goldilocks."

He smiled. "I didn't want to use the more obvious examples, the questions lawyers raise about our social contract. The ethical viability of robbery, say, if you won't give me food and I'm starving. Or life-saving medication if my own children are ill. The issue of trespass if I need a roof . . ."

"The answer's yes."

"Yes what?"

"You *are* at liberty," Beth said. "I think that's the moral here, isn't it? The three bears make Goldilocks welcome and they live happily ever after. Eating cereal, sharing a bed."

"It's a fairytale."

"That's all?"

"That's all."

" 'They go to the seashore,' " she said.

"Excuse me?"

"It's a tag line from *Never on Sunday*. Melina Mercouri, she plays this, this woman with a heart of gold. And she never works on Sunday and everything ends happily in every one of her fantasies; they go to the seashore . . ."

"It's starting to rain," Ballard said.

A telephone was ringing; upstairs, on the second floor, Simon and Garfunkel sang. A spring storm's thunder rolled. She fought back a rising panic; if she opened her mouth she would scream. He collected his papers and books and stuffed them into his briefcase—the brown leather one with the scuffmarks and strap, with the initials PB on the flap, the gilt of their lettering faded, the scratches on the silver clasp—and knocked his pipe into the ashtray and shrugged himself into his raincoat and, leaving, irresolute, paused.

There was a hall door with a piece of plywood bolted to the top right pane, the plywood painted green. The overhead light in the vestibule flickered and went out. Beyond, the wind increased. Ballard curled his hand around the doorknob as if to steady it. "We're going to get soaked," he said. A newspaper blew past. Water puddled on the stoop.

For years to come Elizabeth would wonder if in that instant she had known what must thereafter come to pass, if she already understood the sequence and its consequence; did she foresee, she wondered, and to what degree solicit and acknowledge or could she have prevented the history between them; would anything have changed at all, or would everything (the whole of it, the beginning and the middle and what she knew was not yet the end) have happened nevertheless? Would it have turned out differently if the weather had not held them there, if somehow she had been standing a quarter

of an inch more distant from his elbow, the smell of his
pipe smoke so acrid, so fierce, her breast at the bend of
his arm? What would have changed, she asked herself,
if that day she had a headache or Charette had come to
class, if the book she hoped to borrow had instead been
on reserve? When she asked him for the passage he had
referred to on Monday about the serpent and its coils in
Lessing and the *Laocöon*, he couldn't remember, he
waved his hand vaguely, he was being an absent-minded
professor which is why he touched her hair . . .

"Are you all right?"

"Yes. You?"

"You're not afraid of getting wet?"

"I'm not," she said.

"No?"

"No."

He waited while Beth turned.

" 'Out of this world.' " She watched him. " 'Anywhere
out of this world.' "

The rain was fierce. They moved as though by pre-
arrangement down the pathway to his car. A siren
wailed. There was no one in the parking lot, or only a
hurrying stranger with an umbrella flapping, braced
against the wind. The frog pond looked like corrugated
metal. Its surface heaved in waves.

Ballard unlocked the car for her and, with a dazed
quiescent yielding, Beth settled herself in the passenger
seat and raised the wet hem of her skirt. He turned on
the engine, the wipers at high. They did not speak. It
crossed her mind then fleetingly that what she saw in
him was fear; this was not something he did often or had

done before. The car windows steamed. She was grateful for the weather and the curtain of the rain; and, keeping her back to the window, she pulled her cap over her hair.

Tall elm trees on the campus drive looked black, their leaves upturned, and when he drove her out the college gates and through a covered bridge and past a house she recognized and then down empty water-sluiced and steaming roads and then dirt lanes she knew she had not traveled, and then up a path where the rain seemed to cease because pines crowded thickly, and suddenly a barn was there, its slate roof gleaming wetly, and suddenly they were inside and she was in his arms, he hers, she felt as though there were no choice, no possible alternative, none, none.

II

LOVERS, THEY WERE secretive; he made it clear from the beginning that his colleagues should not know. By their second meeting he had established the rules. "I need to go slowly," Paul said.

"Of course." There was hay chaff in the air between them; sun streamed through the barnboards' wide cracks.

"I just don't want to be public about it."

"Of course you don't. Not now."

He was visibly nervous; he lifted his hands. "Not yet."

Elizabeth accepted this. She did not like to think that she might be responsible for anyone's unhappiness, or at least not directly responsible, or at least not the proximate cause.

"I want this," he continued, "to be something we do without damage. With no *harm* to anyone, ever . . ."

"Yes."

"And I don't want to hurt you, Beth."

Strange that she should comfort him, that he was the one who required protection. "You don't. Or not in a bad way, Professor."

They were in the hayloft; they were standing by the

cross-tie where she draped her skirt. He loosened his belt; he unbuttoned and opened his shirt. Elizabeth needed to sneeze.

"I mean, I don't *ever* intend to hurt you."

"It isn't a problem," she said. She kicked herself out of her sandals. "I'm free and white and next week I'll be twenty-one. Next Wednesday's my birthday . . ."

He smiled. "Congratulations."

"Yes."

When he smiled like that she knew they were special, and the rules of engagement were rules she could break. She had a secret, a wonderful secret, and it was called Paul Ballard and the way they met. She unfastened her bra clasp; she shrugged the straps free.

"I'm not sure I can handle it." He took off his tie. "I hate to describe us like everyone else . . ."

"Well, don't. It doesn't feel that way."

"I hate to think," her lover said, "what we're doing is *predictable*."

"It isn't. Not for me."

And this was true. She did not like to see herself as a Catamount girl with a faculty trophy, a student who slept with a teacher. On the floor of the barn something scuttled away; pigeons, settling in the rafters, flapped.

"I *hate* it," he repeated. "Not you or me or us, of course, but the way it seems part of a pattern . . ."

"What pattern?"

"I believed I could avoid all this. I was planning to. Had planned to."

Balancing, watching him watch her, she stepped out of her panties—first the right leg, then the left. "But?"

"It's all your fault," he said. "You shouldn't be so beautiful."

And then she put her hand on him and he stopped complaining. Paul was her secret, as she was his secret, and the hayloft protected them both.

The dean had just divorced. The man who taught wind instruments was living with his protégé, a blind fine-fingered clarinetist in the sophomore class. Half the faculty, it seemed, were married to their students, and the other half were gay. But what we do together, Paul Ballard told Elizabeth, is our business, only our business, and it should stay that way . . .

"Do you think we're *predictable*? Really?" she asked.

"Not really, no."

"Or that you've been exploitative?"

He shook his head.

"Like, what's his face, Hal Robinson?" Beth touched his cheek. "It isn't, it's nothing like that!"

Hal Robinson taught Art History and believed in the pedagogical model established by the Greeks. He liked to say that mind and body must both be instructed, and a teacher should influence both. "There's no real dichotomy," he claimed, "no viable distinction between the two: body and mind. What Socrates was after was complete and total intimacy: a rite of passage, right?

The wise Greek saying 'Know Thyself' means know your pupils too . . ."

Hal gave this speech at a faculty meeting, then closed by pronouncing "'*Mens sana in corpore sano* . . .'"

"That's Latin," Paul corrected him.

"What?" They were standing in the hall.

"It's the Roman motto. It's Juvenal, to be precise, and the language is Latin, not Greek."

"Don't be pedantic, Ballard. There you go again, being pedantic."

"Expensive education and free love?" He filled his pipe. "Is *that* the thing we're offering?"

Hal Robinson wore love beads and an aviator's jacket and dark glasses even at night. He served as faculty advisor for the Committee on Special Events; he was sponsoring a Hash Bash and the first Annual Dress to Get Laid Dance. He had established the Gay and Lesbian Alliance and the Catamount College chapter of AA. "Expensive education and free love," Hal repeated. "Hey, that's not bad!"

"I wanted to tell you which language you're using. The 'wise Greek saying,' as you put it, is inscribed on the temple at Delphi. And 'Know Thyself' was cited in Plato's *Protagoras* . . ."

"Get with it, man." They stood by the exit.

"Excuse me?"

"Go out and smell the roses." Robinson turned on his heel.

The month of May was warm. Daffodils and irises had been planted by the administration building, and in halcyon profusion white lilac bushes bloomed. The cherry and apple and dogwood trees broke into blossom and leaf. When Ballard walked out by the frog pond he found Beth on a blanket, reading, lying in the sun. She took off her glasses and shook down her hair.

"What are you reading?" he asked. She showed him his own book: *The Mind and Its Inscape*. "I'm flattered," he said. This was true.

"And how far will flattery get me?"

"Oh, everywhere," he said. "Don't you have a class to go to?"

"Yes." She stood. "It's 'Mythopoesis and Literature' at one o'clock. I'll cut it if you want me to . . ."

That day she read no more. They met a next time, then again, and then—as the end of semester approached—so often he ceased counting. They met by seeming accident in Commons or the bookstore or after a dance performance or violin recital. Once when he was leaving town to give a lecture in Pittsburgh, he found her walking in the village and nearly missed his flight. Ballard slowed and stopped to say goodbye and laughingly Beth opened the door and entered the car and slumped beneath the window so that she could not be noticed and—youthful, acrobatic—lying in the bucket seat removed her shorts.

"What time's your plane, Paul?"

"Ten forty-five."

"And what time is it now?"

"Eight-fifty. Ten of nine."

"Then we've got forever," she said. "Turn right here. Stop the car."

He checked his watch. He did have time. He had an

erection already, and he pulled behind a covered bridge and cut the engine while she bent to him and, opening his zipper, said, "You'll wish I came with you to Pittsburgh. Don't you wish I was in Pittsburgh?"

"Yes."

"Say you'll miss me," said Elizabeth and, bending, unbuckled his belt.

It gratified Paul Ballard that she should be so willing to accept what he could offer and ask for nothing more. He did not, for example, invite her to his house. This was understood between them, a border they established and did not choose to cross. He would do so later on, perhaps, but not to begin with, not yet. He wanted no gossip about their tutorial, no bad jokes about faculty-student relations and irrefutable propositions and Dorothy Parker's old saying that, if all these college girls were laid end to end, it would not surprise her.

For there seemed to be no payment due—no bill, as Beth put it, for services rendered. She waited near the parking lot or at night by the library door. She rose from the meadow he used as a shortcut while walking home from campus, or surprised him on the side roads where he drove. She kept a towel in her leather rucksack to rub the hay chaff off their legs after their times in the barn. And sometimes when he looked at her—her ass beneath him, bucking, her blond hair splayed across her back or hanging to the Mustang's floor or, when they met in moonlight, the way she lifted her arms to him and then the bright rising expanse of her breasts—he did feel like a hero, a modern philosopher king.

"Oh fuck me, lover," she liked to say. "Oh fuck me, fuck me hard."

Years later he would marvel at the ease of it, the ignorance, the blithe assumption on his part that there need be no damage. Years later he would ask himself how he could ever have imagined there would be no price to pay.

"Your parents . . ."

"What about them?"

"How would they feel about . . ."

"Us?" asked Elizabeth.

"Yes."

She stamped her foot. She clutched her ankle in mock pain. " 'Thus I refute Berkeley,' " she said.

He watched her. "What?"

"Your speech about Bishop Berkeley, remember? And how Dr. Johnson, according to Boswell, insisted there was such a thing as actual physical pain? Which is why he stamped his foot . . ."

"And?"

"What they don't know won't hurt them," said Elizabeth. "And when I feel they ought to know I'll tell . . ."

"Will they be angry?"

"No. No more than usual."

"Angry at me, then?"

"For corrupting a minor?" She laughed. "For statutory everything?"

"I'm serious."

"Well, don't be," said Elizabeth. "Let's get serious instead about the population problem. Or a problem like nuclear war. Or General Westmoreland and that criminal J. Edgar Hoover and what to do about starvation and police informers and the saturation bombing of Hanoi."

He liked the way she lectured him—her absolute youthful certainty as to right and wrong. He liked her fierce conviction that the government worked hand-in-glove with industry, that America was racist, sexist, a class-bound society; he liked the way her nipples looked beneath the Toxin emblem on her T-shirt, and how she shuddered, coming, and her ankles and long legs. When she convulsed above him, in the car, or beneath him in the pasture back behind the Catamount gate, he felt young again, incautious, though in truth he never had behaved this way when young.

The second Friday night in June he made a reservation at Equinox Waterfall Lodge. Where they ate was sufficiently far from the college so Ballard accepted the risk.

"It's your birthday celebration," he told her in the restaurant. "And it's official, isn't it, that you're an adult now . . ."

"Is this a proper public date? A meal out in public, Professor?"

"Happy birthday, Ms. Sieverdsen."

"In that case," said Elizabeth, "I'll be your consenting adult."

She was mastering, it seemed to him, the rituals of courtship and how in the course of seduction to seem nonetheless aloof. She had pinned up her blond hair tightly and was wearing pearls and a black silk scooped-neck dress and stockings and looked, he informed her, delectable.

"Is that the same thing as edible?"

"Approximately speaking, yes. You do look good enough to eat."

She raised her foot between his knees and left it there an instant. "Later," she said. "For dessert."

They shared a bottle of Pouilly Fumé and dined off quail and trout. Their waiter was attentive but he did not hover; from their corner table they saw the water-fall. Ballard had been planning to spend the summer in Oxford, at the Ashmolean, and he asked Beth what her own plans were and if she would go home. They discussed her thesis and two or three possible topics and which faculty member she should work with for her senior year and whether they could work together and decided over chocolate mousse it was a bad idea. He promised her a reading list, and of course he'd be happy to talk it all out, but for the sake of their relationship it would probably be better if they maintained a certain intellectual distance while she wrote.

"I don't think I could handle it," she said, and when he asked her what she meant she said, "Your disapproval. I don't think I'm ready for that."

"I wouldn't disapprove."

"Of course you would," she said.

The waterfall had been illumined with blue and red spotlights that played off the rocks, and there were pine trees just beyond the window where they sat. The moon illumined the high peak of Equinox Mountain; the evening air was mild. Over brandy, she declared that she had reached a new plateau in life and what she wanted now was only no surprises. She couldn't bear, she said, to think about their coming separation and imagine him in England while she missed him the whole summer long. She had visited a cousin in California the previous August and their experience of living with the threat of earthquakes had made her admire consistency, constancy—what was the line? she asked, you know the song: let's keep on keeping on . . .

It came to Ballard with the force of drunken revelation that the girl was beautiful and rich and young; it was surprising that she cared for him, and she would travel on. In her present world he might loom large, a big fish in a little pond, but by comparison with others, later, he would fare less well. Why should he not, he asked himself, propose that they continue in the fall?

When she returned to college he was waiting; he called her the first night. There was static on the phone. Ballard spoke about his month in Oxford, and the weather there. He alluded to John Ruskin and the article he had completed on "The Whetted Edge of Occam's Razor"; in the Cotswolds he'd thought of Beth often and wished she'd come along. There's a graveyard, he said, in the town of Chipping Campden where the stones are translucent, or nearly, so what appears to hold up the marble is just an arrangement of moss.

Then he asked about her family, and what *her* summer had consisted of, and she spoke about their "camp" on Lake Huron and how dull the happy campers were and how happy and excited she was feeling to be back.

"Would you like to come over?" he asked.

"Where?"

"Here. To my place."

Elizabeth paused. She coiled and uncoiled the telephone cord. All through the previous semester he had not asked her to his house. "You mean it?"

"Yes. I've missed you, Beth."

She stood at a crossroads, she knew, a turning on the map they'd drawn: they could continue or stop. The light in the hallway booth flickered. "The plane was late, I've been unpacking . . ."

"Bring your toothbrush . . ."

"Really?"

"Really. Or don't bring your toothbrush. Use mine."

There were voices in the stairwell. "I have to call my family. I should tell them I arrived."

"All right."

Still she hesitated. "I need to tell you something, Paul."

"What?"

"I tried out an affair," she said. "Last month."

"Oh?"

"He had a motorcycle. It was romantic, I suppose, or he wanted to make it romantic. He was a graduate student, and I thought it would make me forget you. My parents know his parents."

"Well, did he?"

"What?"

"Make it romantic?"

"No." Two girls she did not recognize walked down the corridor, carrying duffels. "It didn't work," she confessed.

"I'll be at the college gate in twenty minutes. See you then."

And she did go to meet him and he drove her to his home. Outside they paused a moment and she heard the sound of crickets; moths battered at the naked light above the kitchen door. Ceremonial, he kissed her, then passed his hand over her breasts. When she stepped across the threshold she felt as though he carried her, and in the living room and dining room as though she were his bride.

In the library she sat. He had lost weight. He smelled of tobacco and Old Spice and sweat. He held a bottle in his left hand and two glasses in his right. Fleetingly, as he approached, she looked up at the window and saw her own face—a trick of light reflected or the imprint of old memory, for she had watched him in this very chair and reading his copy of Alfred North Whitehead not twelve months before. Ballard closed the study curtains and she lay down on the couch.

He sat by her side: they embraced. She turned off

the reading-desk lamp. He was clumsy, a little, untying his shoes, and the brown line on his upper arms where the suntan ended made the rest of him look pale. He buried his head in her neck. The room was shabby and endearing and Beth understood, for the first time, her own power over her teacher and how far she had journeyed to return to this house in the orchard where once she had watched through the window with Charette and Dawn. She felt herself start to grow wet. They met, if not as equals now, as more of a matched pair.

"I missed you," Ballard said.

"I missed you too," she said.

As he worked above her, on the couch, and then again later, upstairs in his bed, she felt a rising wonder at how she had found herself here in his arms, how his appendix scar escaped her notice earlier, and how their reunion was passionate, gladsome, and would last forever and ever. When finally they'd had enough she said she needed to unpack, she still had her suitcases up in her dorm room, and he should drive her back.

"Wouldn't you rather stay?" asked Ballard. "There isn't any curfew, is there? Not for seniors . . ."

"No. But I turn into a pumpkin when the clock strikes twelve."

"Tomorrow then?"

"Tomorrow. I promise," she said.

The first frost arrived in October. The fall turned cold and clear. They met in daylight now, not secretive, and sometimes after Ballard's class they shared a coffee in his office or walked in full view to his car. Beth helped him in the garden he had planted in the spring; there were tomatoes and a few spindly ears of sweetcorn and tuberous potatoes and yellow winter squash. He grew pumpkins and brussels sprouts too. When she asked him, once, about his marriage and his wife and whether he had wanted children, he said we were too young. You can't imagine, Ballard said, how young I used to be.

Hal Robinson sponsored his Hash Bash, and the man who taught wind instruments left his clarinetist for a boy who played the dulcimer, and someone hung a banner across the college entrance gates: *Why Don't We Do It in the Road!* Dawn and Charette were graduated, living in Manhattan, and—as a senior working on a thesis—Beth had a single room. Her thesis dealt with Villehardouin, Froissart, Marie de France, and the Children's Crusade. She missed her friends and studied in the library in daytime and joined Ballard in his house at night, first only on the weekends and then after class on weekdays until what they did together seemed less the exception than rule.

As time went on she cooked for him, and he for her, and on Hallowe'en they had another faculty-student couple over for dinner, then went out to Trick-or-Treat. Beth kept her grandfather's belted hunting jacket—the one with bright red patches so it could be seen from a distance—in Ballard's hall closet, and then she left a dress and pair of extra jeans in the upstairs closet, and her diaphragm in his bedside table drawer. They appeared side by side at the movies and the art exhibit opening and held hands in public while crossing Commons Lawn. For this was 1969, and the world was making love, not war; they were coming, as the Beatles urged, together.

"For Thanksgiving," Beth declared, "I'll order us a turkey."

"Us?"

"We'll dress up just like pilgrims. I'll be your Pocahontas."

"She wasn't a pilgrim," he said.

"All right, then, I'll be Goody Proctor. Who shall we have over?"

"Oh, I don't know. It's a little early, isn't it?"

"It's never too soon for a turkey," she said. "I need to order it fresh."

"It's a family holiday."

"Yes."

"Won't your folks be expecting you, Beth?"

"They won't even notice," she said.

"Are you sure of that?"

She stamped her foot. "Thus I refute Ballard," she said.

With stored apples from his orchard and a rented cider press, they gave a Thanksgiving Day party. They played Twenty Questions and Charades and a game called Botticelli where one person chooses a name and the others must guess which character that person represents. Ballard wrote about the phantom limb, phenomenology, the Casuists, and how in Bernard

Berenson the act of connoisseurship and collecting intersected. "There is only one true antidote," he claimed, "to the anguish engendered in mankind by the certainty of death: erotic joy."

All winter there was great shared joy: they made love in the shower stall and lying by the fireplace in Ballard's library. He liked to watch the pattern of reflected flame upon her back, and how her arms rose archingly when she pinned back her hair. Beth was spectacular in firelight, he said. He was pursuing the distinction between *agâpé* and *eros* and how to the enflamed imagination the former term will conjure legs and mouths agape.

She liked to watch him shovel snow or how his breath steamed in the mornings while he climbed out to the porch roof to brush away the weight of what had fallen in the night; she was grateful when, not simplifying it, he talked about the project he was working on or what he truly thought about his colleagues at the college; she was happy just to brew their tea or watch him frown in concentration, reading, or pull at his ear while he wrote. She could not believe her good fortune, she said, in having secured this tutorial, and he laughed and said oh everything I know I'm learning too . . .

In April and in order to celebrate what he called their anniversary Beth brought mescaline to Ballard's house, and a tab of LSD. The night they took the mescaline the sex did feel astonishing; she was inside the head of his cock, she swore, and he was the lips of her cunt.

"I want to ask you something," he said.

"Okay."

"If we keep it a secret between us, if we wait to announce the engagement until after you're finished here, till after graduation, I mean, or maybe next September, will you marry me?"

"No. No."

That spring she seemed preoccupied, uncertain of her thesis, and one evening after dinner decided she needed to focus and spend the night at school. "I'm sorry," Ballard said, and she said, "Don't be sorry." "Is it my fault?" he inquired, and she said, "Of course not, no."

The April night was mild. He drove Beth to the campus where she could pull an all-nighter, then left her in the parking lot and reversed and headed home. Although he too had work to do Ballard found that he was drifting, with no conscious destination, down dirt roads that felt familiar; he stopped at the side of a newly mown path. It had been a year, or nearly, since they'd first made love together when he brought her to this spot. Cooling, the car's engine ticked.

Near the path he saw a second car, its lights off, in the turnaround, and Ballard wondered if this trysting place was known to others equally. At ten o'clock the moon was high, and he decided to walk. Soon enough the hay barn loomed, its slate roof glistening, its boards a weathered silver; the doors themselves were padlocked shut and there was a *No Trespassing, Violators Will Be Prosecuted* sign. In the clearing Ballard sat; he needed to take stock.

This was not a habit or something he did often; at thirty-six he took his own behavior for granted, or at least he took for granted that he would not change. His attention had been elsewhere, outward-focused; the way the subject and object elided and how the viewer's vantage would affect, *effect* the view. But this girl unsettled him, with her class-bred certainties and her desire to alter the world, her passionate assurance that she need not tolerate what he described as compromise and what she called "second-best." They had come to a point where things needed to change; they could either advance or retreat.

He had had wine with dinner, and bullfrogs in the pond beyond were drumming at his ear. Did he mean it, Ballard asked himself, when he had proposed to her, and why had she refused? Subjective or objective in the sudden rush of passion, did he find himself *surprised* or, as Dr. Johnson would have it, *amazed*? Might there be a useful distinction between the two and did he still feel guilty and was she his equal and opposite number and what would happen next? In that rainstorm here, inside the barn, had he been the seducer or seduced? He tried to imagine a future together, and then a future without her, until the solitude she'd broken through seemed barren, unremarkable: a privacy he had no need to keep.

A night owl hooted distantly, and there was a rustling in the grass. He listened to the nighttime sounds—the wind, the crickets and the frogs, and somewhere, indistinctly, what sounded like flesh slapping flesh. A woman urged her partner on, it seemed to him, and he heard their ardent whispering as though above his head. "Please marry me," he said aloud. "Please, Beth."

Resolved, he walked back to the car and opened the driver's door and stood by it, stretching, and decided he would take a piss and, guiding himself, wrote her initials in the road, E S, or started to, was finishing the E but heard a car approaching, the clatter of metal and whine of its engine, and froze. It bounced over potholes, its headlights were skewed. The muffler, perforated, roared.

He withdrew into thistle, the brush by the path, then saw he had not shut his own car door and needed to close it, it hung there ajar. So he stepped into the road again but the oncoming machine was speeding, fishtailing, cornering at maybe fifty and when Ballard came around the trunk—now visible, now reaching—the driver braked so hard he did a figure eight. For it was rubber, dust and steel and time slowed, shouting, to a crawl and what he would remember of the accident had a balletic precision always, a practiced choreography, for he watched with shocked dispassion as the car turned—windows open, the radio on, three heads inside it revolving—and for an instant felt what he would later recognize as mere embarrassment, because in the glare of the headlights he saw his penis limp and flapping, his pants unzipped, and saw the vehicle tilt riding on its two left wheels, avoiding him, avoiding only barely the oak that would have skewered it and then again revolving, more slowly now, volitional, until the right rear fender cuffed him and he slammed against his own car's hood and crumpled and fell to the ground.

And then there was silence, then noise. Then someone above him was bending, saying holy shit, he's dead, we killed him, no, no, he's alive. Don't move him, is he alone, is there anybody else, Jesus H. Christ, watch him move. You ran him down, you stupid fuck, you jacked him like some fucking deer. I didn't mean it asshole well who was the one with the bottle well why'd you grab the wheel why didn't *you* and what do we do now? Let's call the cops, right right. What were you *doing* here, mister, what the fuck was he doing here anyway, asshole, in the middle of the goddam road, don't touch him, call an ambulance, yeah, and there's all this blood on the fender, we got to get out of here, right. In the wide world's roiled trajectory there was white astonished wind.

And then the three men drove away and for time he could not measure Ballard lay by the side of the road. Then there was a flashlight and dark shapes above him, hovering, a man and a woman come down off the path. When he had finished gagging, spitting, and could look at the two shapes again they seemed to be multiple, everywhere, and bundled him into a car. It was a black four-door sedan, with green plush seats, and when Ballard pressed his nose to try to stop the bleeding he understood the danger to be mortal, and for the first time felt real fear. It was a whirling dizziness, a lifting that was also fall, a circling that he could not stop, a clarity and fading at the same time, at the same time, so now darkness arrived while he tried to see light, and came from the road that they glided and bumped along, and they were talking to each other and in hushed tones arguing about what to do with him, Paul Ballard, what does it matter who he is I can't report him, understand, saying what about the hospital I'm late already I need to go home and let's not repeat our transgression and mend our errant ways (so that later, in the emergency room, in his delirium over and over he mouthed the strange phrase to the nurses, the doctors, the police, repeating *my transgression, errant ways,* and never could be certain if the lovers in the car did use those words or if he had imagined them, nor why they chose to save his life, to spare it) lifting him again at last out of the seat, bloody, mangled, spitting teeth, and stopping at the gate of Holbein Memorial Hospital and positioning him at the entrance where the next car or the next would notice, brake, holding their noses, wiping the cushions, holding their hands out, saying sorry sorry but you see what's going down and I can't get him any closer or be seen with you, goodbye.

III

SHE DID NOT believe it at first. She had seen him just the night before, and they had made love after dinner, quickly, not taking off her skirt; then she returned to campus since Chapter IV of her thesis was due the next morning at ten. She met Melissa Saunders at the cafeteria in Commons, and they had a coffee together, and then Beth went back to her room and worked till four o'clock.

She overslept. Although she had missed the appointment and could therefore not discuss it, she dropped off the draft of the chapter at her tutor's office. There was another counselee sitting in the wing chair and staring at the floor. Miss Garber raised her white head when she knocked, adjusting her glasses and smoothing the ribbon that held them in place. "All right, Beth, I'll get back to you," she said.

There still was time for "The Ballads and Blues," so she dragged herself down to the hall in the Barn where the lecture topic was Ma Rainey and Odetta and Bessie Smith. She sat listening to tapes. It was nice to hear the music, the deep-voiced women turn by turn, and then her teacher describing the lyrics as a form of ritual.

Odetta Felious, he maintained, could have been the true inheritor of an important tradition. But she gussied it all up with drums and guitars and now there's only attitude; now what we have is show business only, the commercial imitation of an art form that once was incorruptible but has turned corrupt . . .

"It's not so much question and answer," Elizabeth wrote in her notebook, "as what we call 'call and response.'"

After the lecture she walked back to Commons and waited on line in the snack bar; it was two o'clock. She wanted a bagel and juice. She thought she might go back to bed. But something in the way the air felt when she moved in it, the way the fan above the grill clicked on, clicked off, clicked on again, the respectful hush and wary expectant attention of those beside her in the line, the way they watched her ask for grapefruit juice and pay for it and then spread cream cheese on the bagel—something told her that something was wrong.

"Are you okay?" Betty Harbison asked.

"Sure," she answered. "Why?"

"No reason," Betty said. "I was only wondering."

"When did you hear about it?" asked Melissa.

"What? Hear about what?"

"Oh, shit, I'm late," Melissa said. "I've got to get out of here, bye."

Then Adam Prothero spoke up. He cleared his throat and touched her arm and said there's been an accident. He told her that Paul Ballard had been hurt. We thought you'd know, he said, we just assumed you knew.

When did this happen, Beth asked, and felt a wind

blow through the room, a cold wind, with ice in its teeth, and suddenly she appeared to be sitting, facing out across the lawn, in the one chair by the window with its springs popped and the stuffing gone and a snatch of song from Bessie Smith repeating in her head. Now everyone was talking, a dozen friends were telling her, well, we don't know exactly, sometime before midnight last night.

I hate to see, sang Bessie Smith, over and over, hopelessly.

They said he was alive and had been taken to Holbein Memorial Hospital and his condition was stable, guarded, critical, he was being operated on but he was fine, he would be fine, it wasn't that serious, really, his life hung in the balance, he was in the recovery room.

I hate to see.

The light was bright. Busily they traded third-hand news and, while she tried to swallow, offered gossip up as fact. It was a poker debt, they said, an accident, a case of mistaken identity and someone they thought was a dealer or drunk and something to do with bad drugs . . .

I hate to see that evening sun go down.

What sort of accident, she asked, and they said maybe hit-and-run and maybe there'd been a car.

Elizabeth went to the hospital and presented herself at the desk. There were two women in green blouses with a heart-shaped *Volunteer* on the sleeve, and when she said "Paul Ballard, please," one woman checked the list.

"Are you a relative?"

"No," she said. "A student. I'm a student of Professor Ballard's."

The woman's nameplate read *Marge*. She had dyed red hair and too much lipstick and was wearing pearls. "No visitors," she said. "I'm sorry, dear, he's only allowed next-of-kin."

"But he doesn't have anyone *here*. His family is *dead*," she said.

"I'm sorry, it's hospital rules."

"Well, can't I call him anyhow? Could I take flowers to his room?"

The second volunteer checked the patient list again, moving down it with her ballpoint pen, and repeated. "No. Not in Intensive Care."

So Beth withdrew and stood outside for some minutes in the open air and then went back to the lobby and directly to the gift shop and waited behind the rack of get-well cards until a group of nurses filed by on coffee break, and she joined them and walked briskly past the desk and down the hall, as though she had a destination, as though she knew what she was doing, and took the elevator up to the third floor.

The hospital was small. It was slated for enlargement and improvement, proclaimed the sign; meantime we hope you'll bear with us. She studied the linoleum, its alternating squares of pebbled black and white, and then she studied the wall. There were pictures in the corridor of deer and Christmas trees and houses with smoke coming out of the brick chimneys, all from Miss Jamaica's second grade. There were self-portraits from the fourth grade also: corkscrew hair, round noses, staring eyes.

Then she reached the two white swinging doors that read: *Intensive Care*. Above the doors, in red, a sign said: *IC Unit; Authorized Personnel Only*. At the entrance her nerve failed. She had no uniform, not even a clipboard; she feared she was going to faint. There were small black smoked-glass windowpanes, and men pushing trolleys, and personnel hurrying through. The sign could just as well have read, *Abandon Hope, All Ye Who Enter Here*.

So she waited in the waiting room, watching a fat man with two buttons missing on his shirt, wearing white socks, leafing through *Good Housekeeping*, not reading it, checking the clock, and a woman with a goiter who grasped her handbag with both hands and rocked noiselessly forward and back on the couch, bending from the waist, eyes shut, and a potted rubber plant, and a framed photograph of a Norfolk pine, and a poster of the boardwalk in what she thought must be Rio de Janeiro, a rocky cliff face sloping up above a brilliant sea. Christ blessed the cruise boats beneath.

"Can I get you something?" asked the man. "Maybe some coffee? A nice piece of pie?"

The woman answered, "No."

Beth had brought along her copy of *Medieval Literature in Translation*, and held it on her lap but could not concentrate and did not try to read. At four o'clock she told herself she would remain till six. She positioned herself in the corner of the waiting room where she could watch the hall. At five o'clock her lover was wheeled past. There had been other patients, other arrivals and departures, but a clipboard clattered to the floor and for a moment those who pushed the gurney paused.

Paul Ballard watched the ceiling. He lay flat on the pillow, a strong-armed black man steering, a nurse maneuvering the IV tree, another at his feet. Beth stood. Paul Ballard stared. He was breathing; he would live. But if he recognized her he did not show it; there was no flicker of interest or attention in the eyes above the bandaged nose beneath the new-shaved scalp. And though she did move forward, shocked, reaching out for him, starting to speak, the three attendants and the bundle on the gurney continued down the hall. The elevator doors slid open, and then again they closed.

"What happened?" they asked her that evening at school. "What did he tell you?"

"Oh, nothing."

"Nothing?"

They were having coffee. They were in Commons again.

"How *is* he?" asked Melissa.

She shook her head.

"Can we visit him?" asked Betty Harbison.

"No."

"No?"

"Not yet," said Elizabeth. "He can't have any visitors."

"Except . . . ?"

" 'With no exceptions.' It's hospital policy. No exceptions."

"Did you talk to him?" asked Adam Prothero shrewdly.

She spread her hands. She bit her lip.

"Was he conscious?"

"Yes. I think so."

"Did anyone tell you what happened?"

She had to admit it then. "No."

In the next days, however, things changed. Slowly the patient improved. Little by little he lifted his head; his eyes cleared and his speech became intelligible and he could tolerate food. The concussion was minor, they said. The visible contusions and the broken nose and the cracked ribs were minor matters also; if there's such a thing as good luck in this case—given what otherwise *could* have gone wrong, given the *possible* scenarios—he had been lucky, they said. After the operation on his leg and shattered pelvis he was put into a semi-private room, but the other bed was occupied by someone who shouted at the ceiling fixture, arguing loudly, fitfully, with the doctors and the nurses, demanding to speak to a lawyer, and at week's end Paul Ballard asked for and was transferred to a private room.

The walls were pastel green. There was a window giving out onto the parking lot. There was a pine stand across the field behind the lot. Beth spent as much of the time as she could by his side, during visiting hours when he had no other visitors and sometimes with a group from school and then, as the term wore on and the nurses recognized and welcomed her, whatever time she had to spare in the early mornings and at night.

She brought him his mail from the college and told him the gossip from town. She let herself into his house in the orchard and collected what books he required. He developed a craving for apricots, and she brought him apricots each day. The bruises at his eyes that made him look like a raccoon turned purple and then green and then began to fade. She read to him and fed him and they watched the news together on the television set above his bed; she held his hand and kissed his raw abraded cheek, departing, and on the rare occasions when he seemed to want to, she let him kiss her back.

But it was over, she knew. There was nothing left between them but a kind of embarrassed silence, and what Ballard did not talk about she did not want to hear. The Catamount police asked questions, and so did the dean of students, and so did all her friends. She had nothing useful to say. Once or twice she asked him anyhow if he wanted to explain what happened or tell her how it hurt and wounded him so that she could understand.

"Understand?" he repeated.

"Yes, or try to . . ."

"You can't," he said. "You couldn't."

"I could try to. If you told me . . ."

His refusal had been absolute. He would not discuss what had happened, or why, or who assaulted or saved him, or what the doctors told him would be the course of his recuperation and plausible prognosis; he simply shut her out. It was as though some something irrevocable had rolled away upon the gurney when he was wheeled past, staring, and simply disappeared. And something irrecoverable closed in Elizabeth also: he was a stranger, as she was a stranger, and they had come together briefly but would now stay apart.

"How do you feel?" she asked.

"Feel?"

"You won't tell me what you're feeling. I have no idea what you've been feeling."

"No."

"What are you thinking, I mean, about me? About the two of us?"

"I can't afford to think about it. Not right now."

"I *want* to help. I'm *trying* to be useful here . . ."

"Of course you do. Of course you are."

"Well?"

He turned his face to the wall.

Beth's period was late. It was irregular, often, but this time it was six weeks late and one evening after *Gunsmoke* she returned from her visit to Holbein Memorial Hospital convinced that she was pregnant and would tell him the next morning and ask for his opinion: should she have their baby or not? Did he want her to abort? Her dreams that night were vivid: marching bands and kildeer limping off their nests and a carousel with actual horses in what looked like Monument Park. When she woke up she was terrified, and the child she thought they might have had proved only the dream's afterimage: a pair of upturned palms, a spotting on the sheets.

When Ballard came out of the hospital she drove him to his house and offered to move in and help. Palpably, he shrank from this and told her she should continue her work and not let his trouble be her trouble too, and therefore Beth completed her thesis and submitted it on schedule and went to the graduation ceremony and was informed that the word "commencement" means both a beginning and end; you're starting out, the speaker announced, as well as finishing up. Think of your life as a Möbius strip, an inward-curled pattern or wreath . . .

Then she drank fruit punch on Commons Lawn in the noon sun with her parents, who had brought the station wagon all the way from Michigan for the occasion. They said how proud of her they were, how very proud of what she'd done, and what she'd learned, and helped her pack and leave.

She did call Paul to say goodbye. "I'll miss you," Elizabeth said.

"Yes."

"I'm missing you already."

"Yes."

She used the hall phone, for privacy's sake. Her mother had been helping to dismantle the dormitory room, folding dresses, packing sweaters, stacking books. Her mother was efficient and well practiced in departure, and it would not take her long. "I wanted to tell you . . ."

"Take care of yourself," Ballard said.

"I'm sorry," said Elizabeth. "This isn't the conversation I imagined we'd be having."

"Oh?"

"It isn't, not at all. I thought maybe you'd come to the ceremony—meet my parents, you know, wave the flag. Or we could maybe see each other one more time. I thought we'd be able to tell each other, oh, something *important* . . ."

"Like?"

"Well, something more useful than only 'Take care.' Which hasn't seemed to work too well."

"It hasn't, has it," Ballard said.

She did not want to cry. She blew her nose. Her mother brought two duffels and one suitcase to the hall.

"'Take care,'" he repeated. "What a funny expression. Does it mean 'careful,' I wonder, as in 'be cautious'? Does it mean be 'full of care' or 'carefree'?"

"All right then, I'll write you."

"Yes. Do."

Her mother scanned the hallway but did not see Elizabeth inside the booth and returned to her labor of setting things straight. All day her parents had behaved as

though this were another of their summertime depar-
tures, a reprise of those they used to make from Grosse
Pointe Shores to the camp on the lake and then on
Labor Day the seasonal return . . .

"Soon," she said. "I'll write you soon."

"I need some time," he said.

She could imagine him lying in bed, the shades
drawn, a book at his side. After eight weeks he was well
enough to walk without crutches, with only a cane.
"What are you trying to tell me, Paul?"

"It's nothing you don't know."

"Just say it then." She felt youthful and determined
and abrupt. "Just say goodbye."

"Goodbye."

By this time she was four months pregnant, and the
doctor back in Michigan announced, "It's now or never,
Lizzie. Do your parents know? Do you want me to tell
them?"

"I'll tell my mother."

"You're young," he said, "and healthy: all systems are
go. From a medical point of view."

But all systems were not go. Her mother had been
raised a Catholic, and she could not countenance abor-
tion, and she said we are or ought to be responsible for
what we've done and for every living creature in the
world.

"What about Laos?" Beth asked. "Cambodia?"

Her mother shook her head. It isn't the same thing, she said. No matter what you did and who you've done it with and even though you won't tell me his name—assuming that you *know* it, even, assuming that you know *which one's* the baby's father—I refuse to let a child of mine be party to destruction."

"It isn't destruction."

"Oh?"

"It's a question of what else to do. What other choice I have."

"You leave that to me," said her mother, "with all your talk about Vietnam and defenseless villagers and how we're bombing villages. I don't know what else they taught you in that disgraceful place, but I believe the Golden Rule, and charity starts here at home. Don't try to deny it."

"I won't."

"Good. That's something, anyhow."

"I'm not denying anything."

"All right. That's something. Good."

Therefore Beth brought her child to term in a long arc of forgetfulness, living in her parents' house, sleeping and waking and avoiding, when she could, her father's scornful monosyllabic fury and Katie the cook's disapproval. She herself became a kind of child; she stayed in her room—reading, watching television—for hours every day. With a sustained unfocused inattentive concentration she watched what happened to her nipples and her navel and she studied her ankles and stomach and the texture of her hair; she lay in the bubble bath—

hot first, then lukewarm, then tepid, then cold—in the early mornings and then again at night. She thought about Paul Ballard and what he would say and what he would do if she told him, and decided not to tell. She was twenty-one, an adult, and she told herself each time she woke and every night before she slept that she was in control of things and could make up her own mind.

But her mind was elsewhere, it appeared. Her mind was with Villehardouin and Froissart and the Chronicles, or watching *All My Children* or the CBS six o'clock news. Her mind was not a part of it, and in the sixth month she agreed with her mother and father and signed the release forms they brought her and the papers they prepared. She signed in triplicate. In the final trimester she gained weight uncontrollably and the pressure on her sciatic nerve kept her alarmed and in great pain, and when her water broke and she was rushed to Mercy Hospital she wanted nothing so much as an end to it all, a completion of what she and Ballard began in what seemed a separate country, long ago, and her labor lasted twenty-eight hours and by the end she was hallucinating, screaming, begging the doctors for help. She had a girl—ten fingers, ten toes, a perfect child, they told her—and fell into a deep drugged sleep and woke only intermittently and by the time she truly woke her child, their child, was gone.

Years passed. It was odd how much attention they required in the passing, how the daily press of things distracted her, how *busy* she had been. At first it seemed that nothing was of greater or lesser value, of more or less intrinsic interest than anything else; she could choose to do something or choose not to do it and the result would be effectively the same. Their love affair and its result—for him, for her, for the daughter they made—had been a kind of general catastrophe, a nightmare that was not a dream. Although Elizabeth could not have said from day to week or week to month what she was working on or working for, there always did appear to be some form of occupation.

She worked in concert management and then a drug rehabilitation program based on the model of Phoenix House; she worked in Head-Start Programs in Brooklyn and the Bronx. Then she left Manhattan for an urban renewal project in upstate New York, but the countryside reminded her of Catamount and so she headed west. Then there were rented rooms, or communes, or apartments and a house in Traverse City she'd been half-tempted to buy. There were beds to make and meals to cook and floors to sweep and walls to paint and letters to send and receive. There were petitions to sign.

In 1973 her father had a heart attack and then a stroke and, after two months of brave fitful rallying, died. Her mother married again. It shocked Beth, a little, how rapidly her mother remarried, but Pete Thompson had been a college beau, and he and his ex-wife had known her parents socially, maintaining contact over the years, at the country club or Ravinia, and somehow it seemed foreordained that her mother—still young, slim, coolly attractive at forty-eight—would want and require a man.

She herself did not want one for years. She slept with men, from time to time, and accompanied them to baseball games and restaurants and, once, for a week to Hawaii. If the men were artistic or political, she admired their paintings or poems or how they planned to run for Congress or subvert the C.I.A. If the men were apolitical, she watched them ride horses or sail. She listened to descriptions of prowess on the rock face or squash court or duck blind or trout stream or stock market floor. Later, in bed or in the booths of airport bars, she heard out their proposals and loud protestations of need.

The Nixon years became the Ford Administration, and then Ford pardoned Nixon and nothing seemed to change. She hated the corporate ladder, and said so, the capitalist mentality and perquisites of wealth that still enthralled Pete Thompson and, by extension, her mother. The Watergate tapes had appalled her, and Beth despised the naked greed and power-grabbing vulgarity that she suspected years before and now had seen so publicly confirmed.

"It's very easy for you," said one young Republican with whom she had dinner, "you, who've never had to work. You, who had a silver spoon. It's easy to make fun of us."

"It's difficult," she said. "It isn't any fun."

"They do a good charlotte malakoff here. Have some dessert," he said.

And this was how it went with her suitors and friends and companions: avoidance tricked out as assault. If she resisted they pressed the attack; if she accepted she asked herself why. At expense-account lunches or dinners they said, "Why don't we play together, why don't you join me in this game?" and then they made up the rules. Having composed their articles of incorporation and reciprocal trade agreements and Declarations of Independence, they wanted her to sign. Some men she found endearing, and once or twice she wondered if a man that she was seeing would turn out to be someone she could continue to see.

The answer, routinely, was no.

In 1974, at a Fourth of July Celebration Picnic in Amagansett, Elizabeth met Michael Vire. He offered her cold fried chicken and corn; she said, "I'm not hungry," and he said, "Good, that's good." They walked together to the edge of their hosts' garden and, sitting in lawn chairs, conversed. Michael was tall and black-haired and angular and affable; he had attended Dartmouth and majored—or so he declared—in competitive skiing and beer. His mother was Italian and his father a lawyer in New Orleans. He said, "I hate this party," and when she nodded in agreement he said, "Let's get out of here, all right?"

He himself was twenty-nine. After some years as a

freelance cartoonist he had taken a job in advertising, with particular responsibility for the agency's Italian clients. He displayed a comic flair for those accounts that dealt with fast cars and high fashion, and he supervised what turned out to be a successful campaign for leather goods from Italy, with a logo of a cow chewing pasta. *Basta di pasta*, the cow mooed ruminatively, and then there were cross-cut long-shots of models in miniskirts and an Alfa Romeo convertible circling the Colosseum.

This tongue-in-cheek attitude served Vire well; he celebrated *la dolce vita* with an Anita Ekberg look-alike spooning pudding and smacking her lips; he did an animated photo montage of chocolates tap-dancing through Venice and then waterskiing giddily along the Grand Canal. With each promotion in the agency, moreover, each step up the corporate ladder he seemed measurably *less* ambitious and *less* reverent, somehow able both to profit from and mock the conventions of Madison Avenue. His combination of Italian excitability and New Orleans laid-back languor kept Elizabeth off balance and (there was no better word for it) charmed.

The sex was good. He liked to talk about "personal space," and how important it was to respect that space and not use it up by breathing in the other person's air. As autumn turned to winter, they saw each other often. He took her to the opera and knew Leporello's role in *Don Giovanni* by heart; he also liked rhythm and blues and, when sufficiently encouraged or sufficiently drunk at the end of a party, played stride piano with a foot-thumping elbow-flying enthusiasm much influenced by

Jelly Roll Morton and whom Michael called "Big Daddy Fats."

Elizabeth decided that the two of them were kindred spirits—surviving in a system they both had agreed to distrust. When he asked her if she'd care to go to Italy for May, in order to scout locations for and then shoot a series of Ferragamo ads, she told him it does sound like fun; when he said we might as well make it a honeymoon, she looked up from her crossword puzzle (what's a four-letter word beginning with "a," she was deciding, for a woodworker's implement: *awls, axes, adze*?) and asked him, are you serious, and he said never more so, and she said all right, okay then, let's try it, yes, yes.

For some years they were happy, living part-time in Manhattan and part of the time in his mother's old farmhouse in Tuscany. It was near the village of Cortona, in a section that had not yet been discovered or at least overrun by tourists, and Elizabeth studied Italian with an interest rendered all the more urgent by need; the women in the grocery store and men in the fields spoke no English, so she learned the language rapidly and, by the second year, well. By that time she was pregnant, and their daughter Serena was born. The ladies of Cortona made such a fuss over Serena, proclaiming themselves so delighted by her laughter and her dimpling cheek, vying with each other in their vociferous admiration of her beauty and intelligence and character that it took the proud mother more time than it should have to recognize something was wrong.

The child was growing deaf. She had been born with normal hearing—opening eyes when her father approached, rocking contentedly in the cradle or her mother's lap, startled at a sudden noise if something dropped. Her crying was predictable, but she no longer cooed or babbled in the crib. She did not turn her head when music played, or if a door slammed suddenly or when the shutters banged and whistled in the mountain wind. As if in honor of her name she stayed *serene* in thunderstorms and while her parents argued as to whether something should be done or could be done in Italy or if it made more sense to fly back to New York.

They agreed to return to Manhattan, and there in fact a surgical procedure did rectify the problem; what she had, the doctors said, was not congenital or sensorineural but merely conducive, a middle-ear effusion and acute otitis media that had been caught in time. They performed a myringotomy, and Serena healed with the resilience of the young.

"We used to handle this with warm water," said the nurse. "She's going to be fine, just fine."

But for Elizabeth it was as though her world had bottomed out again, as though the hospital were all she knew, and night after night in Manhattan she woke shouting from the dream not of her husband or Serena or even her lost daughter but Paul Ballard on the gurney in the hall.

"It's over now," said Michael.
"What?"

"Your dream. Your nightmare. Whatever you woke up about . . ."

"No it isn't," Elizabeth said.

"Do you want to talk about it?"

"No."

"Oh go ahead," he said. "I'll listen."

"No."

"Other people's dreams are very boring, don't you think?" He was standing by the window. He himself was wide awake.

"I suppose so."

"My *own* dreams," Michael said. "Well of course I find *them* fascinating. But I don't talk about them, do I?"

"No. Not often."

"You were shouting."

"Yes."

"Serena's okay."

"I know."

"She won't remember this at all."

"Maybe not," said Elizabeth. "*I* will."

Michael made a movement of impatience. "*Va bene.* Why don't you get some sleep?"

"I'm trying."

"Try harder," he said.

As soon as the doctors permitted Serena to travel, the Vires flew back to Italy. There, safely installed in the farmhouse again, they resumed what Elizabeth thought of as their established domestic routine. Michael, however, withdrew. He slept in the daytime, insisting on silence, then woke at dusk and shut himself into his study at night. At times he looked up from his book or plate or newspaper or cocktail glass and did not seem to notice her or, if he did notice, register her presence. He moved with what his wife began to recognize as genuine indifference from place to place and job to job and role to role; the behavior that at first had seemed seductive to her—his disinterest, his aloof disaffection—lost its charm.

Vire drank. He gave up his partnership and returned to freelance work, fitfully, and then began to paint. She did not like his paintings and though she dared not tell him this he did not seem to care. He was a *dabbler* now, an *amateur*, and these were terms he used, half-smiling, to describe his own efforts in art and at life. He liked to use Rhett Butler's line, "Frankly, my dear, I don't give a damn," and over time he shortened this to "Frankly," or "Frankly, my dear." She had believed he chose indifference as attitude but came to understand in fact he had no choice. He had a bottle of red wine at lunch and a bottle of white wine at dinner and, often, a half-bottle of the strong local grappa at night.

He maintained an apartment in Rome. They had a second child, William, when Serena was two, and for some years Elizabeth was kept so busy with the work and play of mothering that her husband's absence did not matter much. She delighted in her children and devoted herself to their happiness; she wanted to be certain that their childhoods were idyllic in a way her own had failed to feel—that she was always there when needed, always at her children's side, a mother they could count on for support. Reading and writing and painting and horseback riding and sailing were things she could teach them and skills to impart; her children's safety *mattered*, and she never could be satisfied that they were safe from harm. She herself had been so reckless that she needed to protect them, so heedless of impending danger that just to watch them cross a street or mount a pony was a torment of possible risk.

"Don't worry, Mom," they told her, but she said she could not help it; they were precious to her, precious, and she dared not let them break. "We'll be careful," they promised, "we promise," and Elizabeth knocked on wood. For she *knew* about malevolence, how inattention could alter a life, and she made them pay attention to the electrical outlets in the house or the pot of boiling water on the burner in the kitchen or the iron in the laundry where it cooled.

Once her children's schooling started, she spent most of the time by herself. She met Michael on the train from Rome or put him on the plane to America and, since money was not an issue, improved his mother's house. With a part of her inheritance she built a day-room off the living room and enlarged the kitchen; she spent long hours in the garden and grew fava beans and tomatoes and complicated legumes with success.

Among the exiles in Cortona she was famous for fig jam. Her children liked it particularly, and every year when the fig trees were ready they helped her gather figs.

In 1985, when she felt confident enough of Will's ability to float and swim, she had a swimming pool installed on the south side of the house. Serena was dark and lean in the fashion of her father, and Will light-haired like his mother, but they both had Elizabeth's eyes.

In summers she flew with her children to Michigan so they could know their grandmother and relatives and not be estranged from America, and when the time arrived and the decision could no longer be postponed she sent them both, over her own objections and only at Michael's insistence, to the American School in Rome. By the time Serena turned fourteen she announced she preferred to remain in the city and come home only for weekends.

"But what about William?" Elizabeth asked. "How will that make your brother feel?"

"He wants to too," said Michael. "They need a little action, Beth."

"You've discussed this with them?"

By way of answer he spread out his arms. There was no traffic noise. Night was falling on the mountainside and had darkened the prospect already; there were no other lights. A vapor trail above them spread like milk in the overturned bowl of the sky. In the distance she could hear but could not see the plane.

"It's lonely here," Serena said. "It's just too very far away."

"So I'm outvoted," said Elizabeth.

"*Mi dispiace,*" Michael said.

More and more, in solitude, she found herself thinking of Paul Ballard and how and in what fashion things
went wrong. She wondered, did he mean it when he had
asked her to marry him, once, and she wondered how it
would have felt to be his wife. She did not know. She
just could not imagine. She imagined herself at his side.
On a bright spring afternoon in the village of Cortona
she believed she saw him walking—taking pictures of
the view, approaching her across the square and laughing with a friend. The two men wore straw hats. And
though even on the instant she had known it was not
Ballard, known it could not be her teacher magically in
this place and young again (for she was older now than
he had been when first they met, and time would have
darkened him, thickened him, bent him), there was
something in this tourist's gait so much like her lost
lover's that Elizabeth paused, shocked. She passed her
hand over her eyes. When her sight cleared the young
man was smiling at her, strolling by, and he was saying
something to his friend in what sounded like German, or
possibly Danish, or Dutch, and his complexion was
florid, and his teeth were crooked, and he no more re-
sembled her darling than a white pea resembles a pearl.

That night she could not sleep. She had a vision of
Paul Ballard on the gurney, trundling past her in Holbein Memorial Hospital, his hand held out, his eyes unfocused, wheeled down along the corridor where the
elevator doors slid open and then shut. Once again she
had her dream of kildeer limping away from a nest,
feigning a hurt leg by way of distraction so the nearing
raptor would not find its eggs, and then a carousel with

actual horses, and her lost daughter holding to the beribboned metal pole: screaming gaily, laughing in time to the music, kicking her feet in the stirrups and crying out, "Mommy, come *on*!"

Once again she woke bereft. She made herself coffee and stood at the sink, staring out. There were rabbits on the lawn. The telephone rang.

"*Pronto,*" Elizabeth said.

It was Michael calling, announcing he now planned to stay in Rome, saying there was something that they needed to discuss: he and his friend Giovanni were living together and it was time she understood that their marriage was over, *passata la festa,* the marriage had been wonderful, and their two kids were wonderful, *finita la commedia,* but his needs and desires were changing and she must have noticed, hadn't she, how Giovanni satisfied his needs in a way that the family no longer could. The children were fine on their own; they could handle it, he said. Life is a series of stages, said Michael, or anyhow it ought to be a series of adventures and she herself was welcome to remain as a kind of non-paying permanent tenant in the house in Cortona but of course must understand it was his mother's, his family's house, and this summer he and Giovanni would like to use it for August and perhaps put in a tennis court and enlarge the pool. She had been planning, hadn't she? to go back to America for the summer on Lake Michigan and while she was away this year he intended to make some improvements: the turnaround, for example, on the driveway had washed out. He had considered paving it but a runoff with a gutter made more sense.

Elizabeth was unsurprised. She felt even, a little, re-
lieved. The mailman arrived on his moped noisily, slip-
ping letters through the slot. She finished her coffee and
rinsed her cup. She would find out where Ballard had
gone.

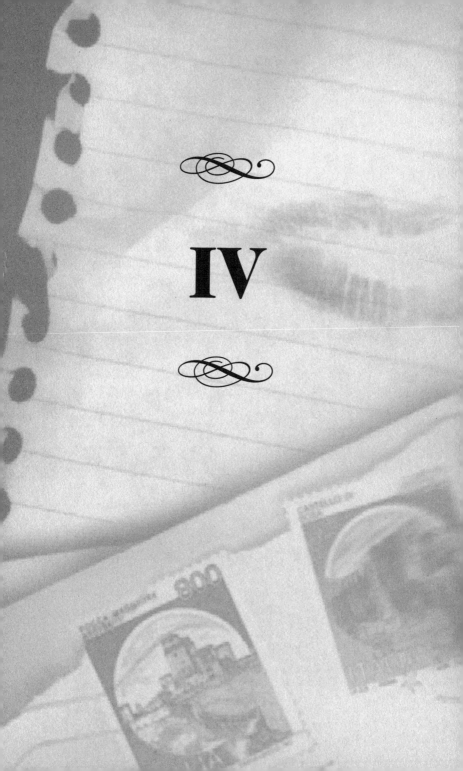

IV

June 14, 1974

Dear Elizabeth:

This will be a long letter. This will take some time. The account of it, the history and record of our sorrows is inscribed upon my memory and even on the ceiling and all across these prison walls, so why not on the page?

All right, it's not a prison wall, and I'm being melodramatic. But it does feel that way. It feels as though the ancient way is the one I follow and as if there were no choice. As though the lines were *written* and the trail already *blazed* and I, who haven't tried to write in years, must use words like "sorrows" and "prison" in order to write you at all. Nor do I know when you'll receive this, or whether, and must offer it up like those passenger pigeons they used to use as messenger—entrusting the bird to a westering wind and hoping it will land. Do you remember Alcuin, his description of the "bird of life" flying through an open barn, flapping briefly from darkness to dark? A sparrow dazed by light? Well that was how you made me feel and how I feel today.

But example is better than precept, they say. My sufferings are worse than yours—a strange sort of boastfulness, really—and should we choose to weigh out our sorrow there's a thumb on my side of the scale. By rumor things go hard for you, and I compose these lines to prove that they've been difficult here too. This is what we mean, perhaps, by "Misery loves Company"—except I've never understood quite what that saying implies. Does it suggest that "misery" takes pleasure in the company of *les autres misérables*, taking comfort in the suffering of others who suffer equally? Or might it mean instead that what we hunt for in our sorrow are those who seem otherwise happy with life—so that we may render them unhappy in their turn? By, as it were, contagion. We're told glee can be infectious; why not misery as well?

So silence seemed the better part of valor; there was nothing new to say. I brought out a pencil and paper and stared at the blank, forbidding page and then simply put it away. Not even a postcard, not even my name; I just couldn't manage to write.

And though everybody and his brother, everyone, everyone, *everyone* has a story that they want to tell or story that they want to hear I felt what I can only call— not horror so much as—revulsion. Not at confession, of course, but at the whole process as such. For four long years I've had the strongest desire to have nothing, nothing, *nothing* more to do with any of this, all of it, the busy-ness of writing, the desperate *me, me, me, my, my, my,* the knee-jerk habit of communication with intimates or strangers or the whole ruck of humanity between . . .

At first it seemed I shouldn't write, and then I thought I might as I grew stronger, but there was just too much to say, too long a list of things to tell, and I couldn't bring myself to do it and didn't have the strength. Then, as strength returned—little by little, a matter not so much of days or weeks or months as *years*, and even now I'm weak, I tremble—there was nothing to convey.

You remember, however, a certain—what shall I call it?—stubbornness, a way I had of sticking with a problem until it could be solved. You used to tease me about it: lighten up, Ballard, you'd say.

And therefore every single day (at different and propitious moments, sometimes before breakfast, or directly afterwards, often in the afternoon and, rarely, very rarely in the evening after dinner) I'd take out a notebook or new sheet of paper and attempt to trick myself (a new pen, an old one, a well-sharpened pencil, a typewriter, a sheet of twenty-weight bond or foolscap or perhaps a lined yellow legal pad) and place these cunning instruments beside me on the desk. Or on a telephone book, or maybe on the window-ledge. Or just on the edge of the chair. Out of old unbreakable habit I believed myself your teacher still and decided you should learn about this chief of sinners so as to lessen your own sense of—what shall we call it: guilt, sin? In writing about my own trouble I sought to alleviate yours.

I scratched XXXX, then Y. I copied the newspaper, copied the psalms. I wrote out the alphabet laboriously—in upper and lower case, both. With my left hand I worked my right fingers and wrist, and then with the right hand massaged the limp left. I practiced my penmanship: first the block letters, then script. Sometimes this took minutes, at other times hours—but every time I tried to write I ended by tearing it up.

They tell me it's predictable; they call it a form of denial. Selective memory. But whatever they name it and however predictable all this might be, I couldn't bring myself to look back at the—what shall I call it?—accident, *incident* and, by describing, relive it. Not even for you, darling, not even you.

Still, I try. Lately when I wake, or walk—I'm pacing the room, I've just finished a turn in the garden—it's much the way it was before: the old professorial impulse to articulate, elaborate (note how those verbs serve as adjectives also) in an audible desire for self-justification, the time-worn habitual need to *explain*. Bear with me while I try.

It happened on Thursday, remember. It happened one late Thursday night. At nine o'clock that evening I was doing what I liked to do, and you seemed to like it too, and we'd had wine and escargots, and God was in his Heaven, and all right with the world. Do you know the line in Browning's poem, *Pippa Passes*—with its muscular optimism, its perhaps tongue-in-cheek conviction that all manner of thing will be well? *God's in his Heaven; all's right with the world.* Well, by eleven o'clock the same evening, not even that hearty bluff poetical Victorian would have been tempted to smile or—at least from this particular vantage—announce that all was well. It's an old, old story: when at last they throw the book at us, it's the Book of Job.

What I remember to start with is darkness. And silence. And then what was no longer the roaring in my eyes but the idle humming of an engine—neither the car that ran me down nor the one that brought me in but some other motor at some other pitch—and the implacable revelatory downturned glare of what were most probably headlights. Too bright and high above me to be a hand-held flashlight or a pocket lighter or a match. A pickup truck, I think, or possibly a high-raked van driven by someone using the back gate of Holbein Memorial for the midnight shift. (Do they call it the graveyard shift, I wonder, or are they superstitious in a hospital and is that *strengst verboten*?) At any rate some Good Samaritan—going or coming, I never found out, on the way to work or on the way back home again (it had to be an employee, or maybe the night watchman, because no private citizen would use that entrance at that hour)—noticed me in the fetal position in the bushes by the stop sign, and stopped and knew enough to know I was alive.

There might have been two of them, lifting me up; they might have called an ambulance. They might have placed me on the seat and hauled me the final few yards. Perhaps they used a stretcher or sent out an ER team. When a wound is too extreme to bear, the body, apparently, goes into shock as a form of self-protection—rather like a circuit-breaker or an overloaded fuse—and so I can't remember how I found myself inside. All this is blank, a part of what I can't distinguish and for the next few hours—the next days, possibly, so much a vagueness I lost track of time—I drifted in and out of consciousness or what we label consciousness so what I remember are images only, discrete.

There's a reddish brown filter in front of my eyes.

It is, it develops, my blood.

There's the unremitting siren.

A suction pump. I do remember this, a suction pump.

There is the perfect parallelepiped of beauty marks (why do we call them by that name? it's curious, isn't it, how what one culture describes as *beauty* another will decry as *blemish* . . .) on the forehead and two cheeks and chin of someone who leans over me and asks is everything all-right, asking if I can hear her and understand her questions and who's the President of the United States and what day of the week is it, what is my name, profession, date of birth, and if I am thirsty and if I can blink.

A doctor, one supposes.

Female. Her hair in a bun.

Not you. I did understood that much, Elizabeth, not you . . .

Nor anyone I knew.

Neither the three who hit-and-ran nor the two who stooped to save (unwillingly, I grant you that; I think what I heard on the drive down to Holbein was the man saying he couldn't be responsible, wouldn't admit to a jaunt in the woods. With a lady not his wife. He'd had his fun; he wanted no part of the police report and would not act as witness or claim the role of rescuer. I've had, as you can imagine, a good deal of time to imagine all this. To try to reconstruct the things they said, these *dei ex machina* fresh from sex. But I cannot see their faces or hear their voices clearly, and should I wish to thank them on the rare days that I'm grateful I would not know who to thank.)

Yet certainly I can remember pain.

Amazing incessant and absolute.

Pain.

There are many degrees and stages of this particular sensation—low-level pain, or constant, or acute, or pervasive or local, metaphysical or physical, to list just a few—and almost overnight, it seemed, I became a specialist in each. Able to distinguish, say, the rising curve from the descending, the unbearable anguish from what can be endured.

An adept of the particular as well as the general ache.

Like the tongue that seeks out the old familiar abscess in the tooth, or finger that presses a bruise.

And fortunate indeed are those who cannot remember the wounds they have borne.

Except as metaphor.

For who among us would survive extreme suffering were the body retentive, the recollection actual; when cold we can't remember heat, when hot cannot feel cold. Just so, alas, with pleasure, although there are several who argue that it's more intense since fleeting, and agony if unremitted must drive a sane man mad.

Therefore I *remember*.

A dietitian.

A priest.

The police.

A way the light played from the fixture in the hallway on the ceiling of the room.

The dawning suspicion that somewhere down there across a continent of sheets, on the far shore of the great inland sea of my bed and at a distance greater than could possibly be compassed by one body (for one of the first things we notice when ill is how the world shrinks in a hospital, and how through the paradox of microscopy or enlargement by reduction a detail that might before have seemed irrelevant looms sizable instead) arose a white-swathed mountain-range of what appeared to be toes.

Dissevered from my ankles?

Could I move them, did they bleed?

Would I eat again, or talk, or breathe without assistance; could I blink my eyelids if I failed to focus on the act of blinking?

The wounds were minor, it developed, and healed without much trouble — surface abrasions, mostly, the things you saw: a broken nose, a broken wrist, a concussion that they feared was worse and told me I was fortunate. Except for the crushed pelvic bone.

The ischium, the ilium and pubis.

My leg, my leg, my leg.

Except for what they could neither measure nor assess: the sense of guilt, the sense of shame, the fear that somehow I had brought this on myself, on you, on *us*. That I'd taken you for granted till you were not there to take. As if you and I prefigured that other couple in the wood, the ones who followed where we led and whom I must have overheard while sitting by the barn. The way they urged each other on, the way they argued, afterwards, as to public attestation, reminded me too much of how I'd been with you before. And it was embarrassing, darling, it was all so damn predictable, it made me feel a fool. . . .

Do you know Flaubert's great line: "Language is a kettledrum on which we beat out tunes for bears to dance to, while all the time we dream we move the stars to pity." It did seem that way to me. I had thought we were remarkable, the single pair of lovers in the verdant world. Yet what I woke to in the hospital was the annihilating certainty that we formed part of a parade of those who fornicate together and believe themselves original: love's old sweet song repeating, repeating . . .

Pain.

Bone fragments, a replacement rod, a series of tubes taped in place.

And that the only way to mend again was through a total break.

Of which more later.

Tomorrow, perhaps, when I'm less filled with self-loathing, more willing to write it all down.

June 15

Dean Fulbert made mistakes. He was a self-important person, not stupid, and he blundered on and on about abstractions that might once have been concrete. Using words like "honesty," "sincerity," "fidelity"—the kettle that calls the pot black. Making phrases like "You have to take charge of your life."

He had been Dean for fifteen years, and much had transpired of which he was ignorant; many things had changed. Still, he conducted what he liked to call an "entrance interview" for incoming faculty members, in order to acquaint them with what was and was not acceptable. I joined the faculty in 1966, remember, a year before you too arrived at Catamount and long before that rainstorm in 1969. There were four or five new hirelings that season, and our topic consisted of, not to put too fine a point upon it, seduction: the old in-and-out.

Quod licet Iovi, non licet bovi. That which is permitted to Jove is not permitted to his cattle.

Or, what God can take for granted ain't available to cows.

Dean Fulbert himself was married to his third Catamount girl, in the process of divorcing her because she ran off with a potter. He was nearing the end of his teaching career and well past the end of his wits. For was not the school's intellectual mission a variety of "hands-on" education?—"Learn by Doing," as John Dewey wrote . . .

Fulbert dribbled; he drummed on the table-top; when not speaking or clearing his throat he nodded and half-shut his eyes. His previous marriage had gone on the rocks because of the rocks in his glass. The ones that he covered with Scotch. And he had been drinking that first afternoon; while he instructed us you could smell the high acetone odor of liquor on his breath. This happened in his office and it happened every year; he would schedule a session with new arrivals in which he warned us, in effect, that we should only fuck those boys and girls we respected and therefore—as a possible prelude to marriage—would choose to fuck again.

I myself had been more innocent than you perhaps imagine; I had focused on my work. It might never have occurred to me that teachers would sleep with their students except for the exemplary behavior of our Dean himself. Well, let me be honest; it would have *occurred* to me but I would not necessarily have put such a theory into practice—even though the Romans were doing each other routinely in our particular Rome.

For three years I avoided it; I needed no confessor and had nothing to confess. I loved the mind's work, Elizabeth, as you will acknowledge, and was completing *The Mind and Its Inscape,* absorbed by that long argument and bent on a career. By 1969 I thought I had embarked on it—attained a certain velocity, even—and others agreed. Then too, by '69 I'd reached the middle of the road of life, that Dantesque turning in the wood, the dark and muddled track. So now that I look back at it the whole thing seems predictable: I was prideful and primed for a fall.

And now I come to think of it, I think it also had to do with how alone I felt those years, the way my parents' death had made me not so much a solitary as a kind of adult orphan. My father went first, you remember. Going down the stairs, he fell and wrecked his hip and did not survive the operation, and two weeks later my mother had what the administrator of her unit called a massive stroke. I believe it was pure plain sorrow, the shocked recognition that she'd have to go it alone. She didn't want to. She simply stopped. So I who had been anchored by my family found myself adrift, though I'd pretty much lost touch with them—oh, I'd been dutiful enough, making phone calls and sending birthday cards and presents and going to the retirement community in Coral Gables for the holidays. But until they died there'd been at least this *notional* and supervisory presence, this sense that somewhere out there adults watched. . . .

At any rate, and for all practical purposes, Dean Fulbert set us both up. He assigned me to you, you to me. I had eight other counselees, for a full complement of nine, and every week for forty-five minutes apiece I met with each of you in programmatic intimacy. This was time-honored practice at Catamount, remember, a tradition of which we faculty members were invited to be proud. An unstructured yet scheduled encounter during which we were urged to *connect*. To know is to grasp is to have tactile experience of is to know: so ran the syllogism. Most often nothing came of it: a tongue-tied post-adolescent discussing his or her problems with the paper due that Thursday on Hemingway or Hobbes, a yawning adult sneaking glances at his watch . . .

And this was how it went with my eight other students—those names on the sign-up sheet outside my office, those Thomasinas, Dicks, and Harriets (the school was co-educational, of course, but I seemed to be teaching two Coeds for every Ed) who arrived to shoot the breeze.

It's a strange expression, isn't it, how would one "shoot the breeze"? Does it mean "miss the target"? or simply that our marksmanship is foredoomed to failure or that the hot air blows past? I remember sitting hour after hour, watching the leaves drift down, or pollen, or snow, and searching for something to say to these counselees, some topic we might explore in common for the allotted time-span: forty-five forced minutes every week. We were supposed to catch up with each other and talk. *How is your boyfriend, your girlfriend, your family, your experience of Dostoievski, your reading of Heraclitus, your plans for the winter, the summer, the trip to the Bahamas, the prospect of graduate school?*

It won't have escaped your attention, Elizabeth, that I'm backing and filling this paper with prose. I follow the lead of doddering Dean Fulbert and advance by indirection; I'm saying very little here and doing so at length.

That we were foolish I freely acknowledge, that we were wrong seems less clearly the case. Do you remember Abelard's *Historia Calamitatum*? — "We entered into each new joy the more passionately for our previous inexperience of passion, and were the less easily sated." The two of us consulted in my office, or in fair weather walked together while we discussed your problems, both academic and personal. Your studies allowed us to withdraw in private, and whatever I devised you welcomed; the reverse, too, was the case. What had seemed like mere inconsequence became consequential instead. And so we were united, first under one roof, then in body, then in heart.

For in handing you over to me to supervise as well as teach, what else was Fulbert doing but offering me the freedom to realize my desires, and providing an opportunity for me to bend you to my will? If he had entrusted a tender lamb to a ravening wolf it couldn't have tempted me more. Before our books and notebooks were open, I urged you to take off your clothes. There was a good deal more touching than teaching; we scrutinized each other's bodies as our texts.

But example is better than precept, *verdad*, and therefore I'll get to the point. In my youth I thought it lust, yet now I understand how, lost, it may transmute to love, and how much greater finally is the conjunction of the two: part fitting the ragged-edged part. And how astonishing that there should be, whether preordained or earned or found by accident, a second self, a partner in desire.

For what you need to understand—what I have to make you understand—is that none of this is automatic; everything was choice. Not chance. What we did for those twelve months we entered into freely, and of our own free will. At every moment I could have insisted, "Thus far, and no further"; we could have called it quits. All that talk about determinism and the involuntary act, all those discussions of biology and imprinting and the logic of predestination—all of it misses the point. The point is we could have said No. The point is we both said Yes, yes.

And what were we after, my darling, what notion of perfection held us in its thrall? What Platonic ideal— though we were scarcely platonic as lovers—did you see in me, I you? As though we were component halves of the one whole? Why couldn't you leave me alone, why didn't we stay separate; what was I thinking of, what?

Do send me (though I wish it were the opposite, and you could be here in my arms) a sign of flesh made word.

June 16

Today is yesterday's tomorrow and I shall try again. It's difficult. My besetting limitation, as you above all others know, is how hard I find it to be easy, how complicated to be simple, so that even such oxymoronic pairings as these become a kind of formula: intelligent stupidities—my pretty *mots* all in a row. Because the irony of what happened on that Thursday night was just too obvious: man makes up his mind to get married and thereafter is unmanned. Man decides to do the "honorable" thing and a quarter of an hour later might as well be dead. And cannot bring himself to ask out of weakness what he had hoped for in strength . . .

So I'll try once more to tell you, even though I've failed before, and to tell it straight.

There were orderlies and nurses and pathologists and neurologists and urologists and anesthesiologists and volunteer workers and people with mops. You visited also and did what you could, but there's no egotist like a patient, or at least this particular patient, and I remember everything, although it happened years ago, as though it were yesterday, happening *now*, as if it were, *is*, present tense. There appears to be one of the medical people to whom others defer; there's another nurse practitioner most often at my side. Her name is Rose. I try to make a joke about a rose by any other name; it does not work. Remarks, as Gertrude Stein averred, are not literature. The joke, I mean, falls flat.

Nonetheless she makes me walk, negotiating corridors, clutching to the life line of the IV tree. And counting linoleum squares.

For when you start to look for it you find a pecking order everywhere: a hierarchical arrangement of the orderlies and the ICU personnel, the ladies by the coffeepot, the minister and rabbi and trainees or experts from Rutland or Albany, with all of them negotiating rank.

So this too partook of gradation and the degree of — it's a medical term, Elizabeth — *insult*. To the body as much as the brain.

A Dr. David Horowitz arrived to see me often. He had been my chief surgeon, apparently, though I could not remember either his presence or face. He had that bluff brusqueness that seems to be a *sine qua non* of the specialty, as if surgeons learn to calibrate with professional exactitude how many seconds and minutes they must allot to what the rest of us describe as life.

The back-and-forth of conversation.

Human interaction. The kind that requires no knife.

He was thirty-three, perhaps. Bald already. Whippet lean.

A jogger in his off-time, as so many doctors seem to be. And no doubt working up to his first marathon.

Unmarried. Engaged. Preparing to tie the knot and

hitch the hitch with his Rebecca as soon as she completed therapy and he had paid off his indebtedness and earned 100K.

Dr. Horowitz made small small talk, however; he studied my X-rays and body, not face. His "bedside manner," as it were, was not calculated to inspire confidence. So it took me longer than it should have, possibly, to understand what he was saying and what he expected.

A full recovery. A reconstruction that pleased its principal architect and prime mover no end. A degree of pain in the pelvis and leg that would be difficult at this junction to predict and likely to be life-long but something I could no doubt live with and in any case must learn to and that could be monitored and thereafter controlled with medication. A happy ending, a surgical triumph, a success.

Success?

Nec quia Deus id dixerat creditur, sed quia hoc sic esse convincitur recipitur.

We do not believe a thing because God has said it, but because our reason convinces us that it is so.

Had my bladder been full when my pelvis was fractured, for example, nerve damage in the area would likely have been greater and I might prove incontinent. *Per contra*, had I retained a full bladder I might well have been uninjured. Which lends a certain ironic urgency, as I did not tell Dr. Horowitz, to the instructive apothegm: *Don't piss away your life.*

I will not, I won't send this, I can't. I'll tear it up in the morning, I promise; this is a letter not sent.

When we read an argument or listen to a speech, it's hard for us as witnesses to draw the line between an actual and a simulated modesty. To decide when that modesty's genuine or false. Whether the *aw-shucks* attitude and downturned self-deprecatory smile be authentic or feigned. And all of this grows much more difficult, of course, when one's subject is the self.

So a lie if repeated sufficiently often becomes remembered fact.

But for my own part I'm unsure at what point the modesty's actual and when I merely simulate the stance.

I write you this, however, in what I believe to be the spirit of humility.

I did make mistakes.

Not to mention my own disordered sense of what in fact happened that night. My hallucinatory certainty that there were brass knuckles involved. There's a kind of clarity that washes over us in times of great peril or stress, perhaps, but also a kind of confusion—and this is all I can remember, darling: the soft contour not hard edge of shock.

Who were they?

Would they be found?

Tracked, caught, identified, arrested?

Shot?

Yet even dreaming of revenge, even in the first fevered weeks, I think I knew the names of those young thugs who almost killed me were beside the point. And that the punishment they meted out was, in the final analysis, self-inflicted; it was as though I'd brought this beating on myself and the hand, if not of God, of some unforgiving judge were evident in bruise and broken bone. From metatarsal to metacarpal, and each of the stages between . . .

For every incident there must be a prefiguring accident, a sequence of inconsequence, both cause and prior cause. This is what I've always argued *is* the dialectic, a fusion of paired opposites—not Hegel's thesis and antithesis so much as the electrical attraction of plus and minus charge. And this is what the credulous would call divine intervention, perhaps: I'd been permitted to wander thus far and no farther and was by their arrival brought back.

It's a peculiar sort of providence, admittedly, but providential nonetheless. As though I tried to cross a street and someone runs the light and knocks me to the pavement and I therefore fail to reach the side that, before I attain it, blows up: a shell exploded precisely where I'd been intending to stand. Or as though I failed to notice how the roof of the arena was about to buckle while I sat and watched a game, and so I went and bought a hot-dog or perhaps a beer and made a call and while I was away for only an instant a girder crushed my seat . . .

It was, I mean, machinery and not my three assailants that broke me so entirely into component parts. There would have been no malice aforethought—no *thought* at all, a thoughtlessness. And in that way the accident seemed, how shall I put it, *impersonal*. We see this happen more and more often nowadays, an act of blind indifference, the human engine stalled. As though it had nothing to do with me in particular but with everything in general about the way we both behaved.

In the literature of phantom limbs we read with regularity of those who lose a hand or leg and dream that they can grasp or walk with the missing appendage nevertheless; there's pain in the fingers or toes. Nerve-endings, apparently, fail to adjust to such loss.

Therefore it's not surprising that after the accident, *incident*, I dreamed for weeks and months of sleeping with you in one bed, of coming unalone at last, and when I waked I cried, like Caliban, to dream again.

Of which more later.

The reality, I mean, and not the dream.

Bear with me, Beth, it's dark outside and has been dark for hours; I shall resume this in the morning.

If I can.

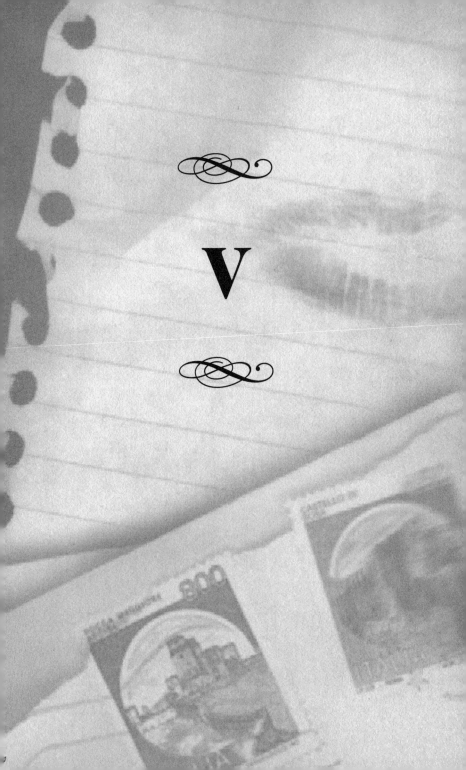

V

A SILENCE FELL upon the land, or so Ballard believed, and he embraced it gratefully. There was nothing he wanted to say. In Holbein Memorial Hospital and during the long period of recuperation thereafter he could find no use for language: the less said the better, the least best. Discharged, he did not want to think about and therefore did not talk about or write about the past.

For the first weeks the telephone rang, but he did not answer it, and he made no calls. Renouncing her, and consciously, he sent Beth Sieverdsen away. Pain was with him always, and at times did feel remarkable, but there was nothing to remark about it that did not sound self-serving. There was no one he wanted to see. When visitors knocked on the door unannounced, he endured their conversation and ate their proffered casseroles and drank their fruit juice or whiskey and wine; by way of speech he nodded or, frowning, shook his head. He did not invite them back.

This went on for some time. Because of the extensive nature of his injuries, he was placed on medical leave of absence from the college; Irene Garber took over his class. She had been planning a sabbatical, but it could be deferred. He watched the apples in his apple orchard ripen, fall, and rot. He watched them in the early spring break into blossom and leaf.

In September of the following year he did return to teaching, but it did not work. The pain would start and spread and fade and flare until what he took to control it was controlling him instead. Ballard could not remember the texts he assigned, or how to conduct a discussion, or whether or not to give tests. His classroom notes and lectures made no sense. He fell silent for long periods in the middle of a sentence or fiddled so obsessively, lighting his pipe, that a whole book of matches guttered out. He had nothing to report to these bright-eyed or bespectacled or willowy or plump or pale-cheeked or bearded or acne-bespattered children, and he found himself repeating only the first line of Goethe's *Faust*: "*Habe nun, ach, Philosophie!*"

"I've had it with philosophy," he admitted to Dean Fulbert. "I've had enough. Too much, in fact, more than enough . . ."

The dean was drying out. He too had had enough, he said and was planning to retire in the spring. He'd given his all to this place, he declared, and it's the beginning of madness to believe you're indispensable to any institution, or certainly to this one; he himself had no illusions, or rather he'd *had* that illusion before but mostly it came from a bottle. Mostly it was fantasy, not fact. For far too many years he'd fooled himself into thinking that the college would be grateful and the job he did was crucial, requiring his particular and personal attention. Fulbert himself had joined the Catamount chapter of AA, and he sucked gumballs while they talked, twisting and smoothing the cellophane wrappers and sharpening the pencils that protruded from a leather-wrapped mug on his desk.

"I quit," said the teacher, more loudly this time, "I've had it with philosophy," and Dean Fulbert—smiling, nodding, signing papers—did not disagree.

There was a monastery in Argyle, across the New York border, and Ballard paid a visit to the monks. He told them he might want to join. The monastery sat on the north-facing slope of a hillside with a lake and eighty wooded acres that the founder of the order—a retired advertising executive—had deeded his associates in 1968. It had been Brother Robert's dream to establish a community of brethren, and while he lay dying of lung cancer he organized and then endowed that dream.

The original group numbered twelve. Their faith was Russian Orthodox, or a version of Russian Orthodox with an Episcopal emphasis, and they accepted lay brothers and were, so they said, ecumenical. The group had been incorporated as a monastery with an outreach program and as a viable alternative to the Alsatian-raising brethren of New Skete. They were educated men, men who valued education, and now they welcomed recruits.

Brother Everett showed Paul around. Brother Everett was stout, and bald, with a brown cassock cinched by suspenders and a flat-footed splay-legged stride; he had patterned his costume on Friar Tuck. He announced this happily, patting his stomach, telling Ballard that he'd cut and stitched the clothes himself and was planning to market the cassock and thereby take advantage of the new widespread commercial interest in leisurewear. The Nehru jacket—did Ballard recollect the introduction of the Nehru jacket?—failed, and that's because Americans can't see themselves as Prime Minister Nehru but can as Friar Tuck. Or Robin Hood or maybe even Little John.

"You can't imagine," Everett said, "how good a piece of cloth like this can make you feel."

He pointed out the vegetable gardens and the sheep pen and the place they made their famous chocolate cheesecake and their Fancy Maple Syrup, available at wholesale prices in the guardhouse by the gate. There were several wooden dormitories and a chapel and refectory and henhouse and a kennel.

"You ought to take a shot at it." Emphatic, the monk nodded. "Retreat, I mean. Try our experiment on for size."

"Experiment?"

A three-legged German shepherd came bowling unsteadily over, then settled at Everett's feet. He scratched at the dog's ears. "This is Harry," he said. "Harry, Paul." The dog gazed up unblinkingly, then turned away.

Brother Everett finished his tour. With his cassock sleeve he wiped the slats of two green Adirondack chairs and gestured for Ballard to sit. There were linden trees behind them, and aspens rustling in the wind. Crows cawed.

"Up over there," said Everett, pointing, "is where we eat and down there's where we sleep. It's like"—he smiled again—"the whole idea behind insurance, I mean on a *personal* level, you make sure you pay your premium and then you stake a claim."

Once more Brother Everett nodded. His dentures were perfectly white. There were Cistercians up in Manchester, but absolute silence is hard to achieve and he himself preferred the company of like-minded intelligent brethren; there's a premium on silence here except we can break it to speak. Therefore it helps to have companions who were successful in the workaday world but have renounced, like Brother Peter Antonini who had been a lawyer and Brother Charley Morrissey who used to own the second largest Chrysler dealership in the tristate area; believe me, he said, when I say these are strong-minded men, men of strong opinions, and when they start to talk you can bet your bottom dollar it's because they have something to say.

In his own worldly life—that was how Everett described it, his previous and "worldly life"—he had sold insurance. He had been office manager for the All-State Insurance Agency in Greenwich, New York, and was in line for a promotion and was going to be transferred to Glens Falls.

"But then one Tuesday morning, bright and early," he said, "I looked around me—at my logbook, all the calls I made and the visits I had paid and was scheduled to finish by Friday, all the policies I'd sold that month and the problems I'd been dealing with—you know what I'm talking about, Professor, widows and orphans and fender-benders and policies suspended for nonpayment and lightning strikes and liability for milk fever and hoof rot and swimming pools and fire and whatnot—and said to myself, 'Pal, you've been handling the wrong kind of insurance, there's only one true certainty and it's in the hands of the Lord.'"

He pulled out a red handkerchief and unfolded it and, loudly, blew his nose. "I recollect the moment perfectly clearly, the moment when I found it, or maybe *it* found *me* and the word I want is *discovered*, or maybe the real world is *encountered* what—because of my worldly and previous life, understand, because of my workaday ethic—I used to think of as only just another version of insurance. Salvation. The way we've been taught Jesus saves.

"It had been raining that morning and I was in my car." Brother Everett paused. Dogs were barking. Shrilly, he whistled. They stopped. "And I had a call to make in Shushan, an assessment for water damage in a basement, I recollect, and it was maybe the third time this particular client had had trouble with a claim. On this particular day I had a headache and was feeling— one beer too many the night before, it wasn't unusual, it happened to me often at that period—well, *punk*." He shrugged his shoulders, repeating this. "Punk. Then all of a sudden the sun came out and suddenly there was this great humongous rainbow and it looked exactly like a *sign*. It was like my windshield wipers were announcing it, were *spreading the news* and telling me, and it seemed like a kind of *conversion*, how the true pot of gold at rainbow's end is not in the office or somebody's basement in Shushan but up on this mountainside. Here."

"I thank you." Ballard stood. "*'Habe nun, ach ...'*"

"You'll try us on for size soon, right?"

"No. No."

Now what he wanted was silence, unimpeded solitude, and he wanted this all the more fiercely as he continued to heal. He was not uninterrupted, however, or for long periods alone. A woman from the college Publications Office telephoned; her name was Peg Donellen and she reminded him they had conversed once or twice in the faculty dining room, and wondered if he'd care to do an interview about the accident and his recovery and what he was planning now.

Ballard told her, "Thank you, no."

Students dropped by, and colleagues came, and old friends wrote or called to ask if they could be of service and if he needed help. They approached him, always, with a certain caution; they hoped he wouldn't mind. He should feel free to tell them if he wanted company, and they would understand if he preferred no company just yet. Silence is golden, they said, and the process of healing takes time.

He agreed he did in fact need time, and they said yes

of course, of course, and didn't mean to intrude. They asked him if he wanted an *au pair* or maybe a practical nurse in the house, someone to help with the cooking and shopping and cleaning. They knew someone who knew someone whose expertise was clinical depression, and they would be happy to arrange for a referral. They asked him if he thought it might be useful to consult with doctors—with experts, say, in post-traumatic stress or hysterical paralysis—and though they didn't want to meddle they knew experts in the field; would he like to schedule an appointment?

To each of these suggestions Ballard answered no. He wanted his privacy, privacy only, and he made this clear enough so that his colleagues and students no longer stayed in touch. He spoke to the mailman or to the man in the snowplow or grader or discussed the weather with the bagger in the checkout line at A&P or with Mr. and Mrs. Harrington at their store in Shaftsbury. That was all. That was the entirety of his commerce with the world.

He mowed the lawn. He raked the falling maple leaves and shoveled snow and rototilled his garden in May and planted it and tended and then turned it under in October. He maintained the apple orchard with some care. Having canceled his subscription to the *New York Times*, he stopped listening to the radio or watching the news on TV. He took down the hall mirror and in the bathroom, while brushing his teeth, shut his eyes. He accustomed himself to a daily ration of one conversation per day. If he said hello to the mailman, for example, he did not speak to the man in the snowplow or the lady who sold him provisions in the State Line convenience store.

Such silence bred silence, accreting. As though indeed he were a monk or one of the brethren in Argyle, Ballard kept to his house in the orchard and his reclusive ways. The monastery would have been by comparison convivial, its discipline less arduous and its rewards more clear. He grew a beard for seven days, then shaved for seven days, then grew a beard again and marked the calendar accordingly: week by week by month. He drank tea and took his pills. A stray cat appeared and stayed, then left again; the cicadas and the chickadees were what company he kept.

He did, however, play music—Bach, Gesualdo, Palestrina—and throughout his convalescence he practiced the guitar. At first the chords and melodies eluded him but then his fingers loosened and he grew, little by little, adept. He ordered scores from a catalogue: first at beginner level, then intermediate and then, finally, advanced. For Ballard could remember, with a kind of body-knowledge that was not conscious memory, himself in a high-chair conducting, waving his arms while his mother and grandmother applauded. The preludes and gigues and sarabandes provided both challenge and comfort; he performed a transcription of "Air on the G-string," and then the "Agnus Dei" from Fauré's Requiem.

In this fashion he beguiled the time and did not mark its passing. For years he woke up shouting, though he could not tell before he slept what would trigger that night's terror or why he had dreamt what he dreamed.

"Professor?"

Ballard turned.

"Excuse me, Professor Ballard?"

He nodded.

"I don't know if you remember me."

He was standing in the checkout line at Harrington's Grocery Store. He shopped there once a week.

"Sam Axelrod." The man held out his hand. "The 'Ghost of Christmas Past.' We met here before in, when was it, '70?"

Ballard made no answer. He would be next in line to pay, and his food was on the counter.

"I'm from the *Voice Supplement*. I used to write profiles—remember?—and I did that story on Catamount College."

The fire station's siren shrilled, subsided.

"Well, anyhow, Professor, it's a real coincidence. I remember your *Musical Silence*, I read and enjoyed it way back when. That other one too, the one about 'mind.' And I happen to be passing through—we're up here for the weekend—and I found myself, well, wondering, just what you're up to lately. . . ."

Outside, the siren rose and then again declined.

"We were driving up to Sandgate, and my wife wanted a sandwich, you see"—Axelrod brandished a can of apple juice and a tuna-fish sandwich in paper—

"and so I told myself I'd maybe get a chance to say hello. I was thinking I could look you up. . . ."

"Why?"

"Excuse me?"

"Why would you want to look me up?"

Axelrod smiled. He had freckles and a sunburnt neck and dark glasses on a chain. "No reason," he said, "no particular reason." Incongruously, for he was wearing pressed white pants and polished loafers, he sported a soiled Agway cap. "I did want to ask a few questions."

Ballard paid for coffee, bread, sharp cheddar cheese and milk.

"That's if you have a minute free, if I'm not interrupting . . ."

Pat Harrington behind the register bagged his items carefully.

"I heard about what happened here."

"Happened?"

"I mean, my friend Hal Robinson was telling me. About—when was it?—1970. We were talking, him and I, about the way—"

"He and I," said Ballard. He inserted the bag of groceries in his leather knapsack and shouldered it and prepared to leave.

"What?"

" 'He and I,' " Ballard repeated, his pedantry engaged again. "*He and I* were talking."

"Whatever. About that accident of yours. If you don't mind me asking."

"*My* asking," Ballard said. "It's a gerund." He opened the screen door.

"That friend of yours, your *protégée*—wait. Wait." Axelrod glanced at a notepad. "Elizabeth Sieverdsen, am I right?"

They were standing on the store's front step. A white BMW with New York license plates idled at the curb. A woman in the passenger seat, wearing dark glasses, tapped the horn. Axelrod held up his hand. "Hal said you were fired, is that a true fact?"

He shook his head.

"So like I said, Professor, I do have a few questions. I remember what they said about how badly you were hurt and I remember there was talk about, well, about what went down with that student of yours. And I can understand, of course, if you'd rather let bygones be bygones, but maybe we could make a date to talk about that hit-and-run. . . . "

There were two racing bicycles on the bike rack on the car's white roof. The rear seat was piled high with gear.

"Because what *happened* to you is important"—the reporter touched his Agway cap—"even if, and I can understand this too, you don't much enjoy discussing it."

"And?"

Sam Axelrod watched him expectantly. "That history of yours," he said, "it's, like, a part of that whole period. Of our collective history. And I've been working on, or thinking I would maybe work on a kind of, oh, personal memoir. A memory of what it felt like to be part of the crazy scene we all were making . . ."

"Sandgate," said Ballard. "Is that where you were headed?"

"Right."

"Well, if you start now and drive straight up Route 7 you'll just about be there by dark."

Paul Ballard turned forty and then forty-five. Although he played no public role, he did break his silence with letters. When the Catamount Board of Selectmen planned to improve the Whitechapel parking lot and pave and widen Whitechapel Road he wrote to the *Catamount Clarion* about the mandated separation of Church and State. The disjunction of the two, he wrote, is our most precious and enduring constitutional principle, and this citizen would like to see the tar and feather-bedding of those contractors who violate the social contract in so cynical a fashion. When the school board voted to restrict the budget for music instruction and increase the funds for football he sent letters to the board: a society, he argued, is no better than its song. Those who cannot tell the difference between a sonata and a symphony, apodosis and protasis are, he wrote the editor, fools. And this witless subservience to and willing acquisition of uniforms—these funds allocated for cheerleading and numbered jerseys and helmets—is a proto-fascist circumstance we as citizens ought to reject.

His health improved. He passed through fear and trembling and what the doctors assured him were the appropriate stages of grief. On the day of his forty-eighth birthday Ballard renounced tobacco; he broke his pipestems and buried his pipes. And though he woke up some mornings erect, he took no satisfaction in release. What he had done with Elizabeth, and she with him, became a kind of template for that memory palace, the past; he walked himself from room to room and shelf to wall and chair to bed, remembering in detail how his lover had shrugged off her clothes in the barn, or how her mouth moved when she spoke. She was a vivid chapter in a book he wished to close.

On the day of his fiftieth birthday—he marked the date by shaving—a girl appeared out of the orchard and knocked on Ballard's door. She was fighting back crying, he saw, and had grass stains and dirt and burdock down the side of her dress. She was twelve or maybe thirteen years old and stood by the screen like a stork: long-legged already, and rubbing her left leg with her right instep where it itched above the ankle. She was up for the summer, she said, and out riding her bicycle for the afternoon and would be late for supper and was lost.

"You take a spill?"

"Yes." She pulled at her left side.

"Hurt much?"

"Yes," she said. "But not now."

"Well, where are you going to?" he asked.

She told him, and he knew the place, and was impressed by her bicycling diligence; give or take a couple, she'd traveled twenty miles. She was swallowing the road dust and he offered her something to drink.

"I'd like a glass of water, please."

"We can do better than that. Have root beer. Have some cider."

"I'd like water," she repeated. "Please."

He went to the kitchen and drew a glass of water for her, seeing the glass bead. He saw her yellow bike propped up against the fence. Ballard was feeling generous (and knew the generosity not typical, knew even then it was compounded of the afternoon's completed work, the honeysuckle smell in the soft air, the chill of his right hand's wet palm and the suspicion that she evidenced about the glass he offered—her city manners nicely according with this new country necessity— knew that he liked the bravura about her, not tears she had been fighting back, but not not-tears either, and the distance she'd traveled since breakfast, knew also he could circle back by Nickerson's and settle up about the apple orchard and find out what was happening to Tim, knew suddenly the house had held him for too long and why not break a habit and accommodate this once . . .) and offered her a ride.

"I've got my bike."

"I got a truck," he told her. "We'll haul it."

"I couldn't," said the girl. "Thanks anyway. And for the water."

"Put that glass down," Ballard said.

He stepped around her and down off the porch and picked her bike up and slung it in the truck bed and tied it to the crossbar. "Get in," he said, "we're going," and climbed into the cab.

The girl had obeyed him, of course. Yet there was something peremptory in her submission, a kind of acquiescence that made the favor offered seem not his favor but hers. She edged the door shut, and he told her to slam it. She did. He asked her name; she announced it. "Sally. Sally Axelrod."

"And where are you from?"

"New York."

"New York City?"

"Eighty-third Street," said the girl. "Between Park Avenue and Madison. Do you know where that is?"

"Close enough."

"Well, I think it's the very nicest part. Because there's a museum there and I've a real bike, not like that one"— she tossed her head—"and I ride to school if I'm late, or Mary doesn't feel like walking, or for any reason mostly, as long as I wait for the lights."

"And don't get lost?"

"You can't, not really. Not in the city. You'd know that if you knew it well. There's Central Park. There's the East River to the east and the Hudson to the west, and even-numbered streets run east . . ."

He cut across Route 7 and took the old East Road. She sat beside him stork-legged, voluble, pitching her voice high against the engine din, and chattered while he watched, idly, forgetting (if indeed he even saw fit to remember or listen to her singsong litany of how to get where you're going, and her game of naming trees) what else she told him or asked. She asked though, Ballard noticed, to be let off two miles from her house.

"My mother would be angry," she explained. "At me making you come all the way. I can make it back from here, really. Really and truly. I take the first left turning, and then it's just down that hill. Please."

"All right, if you say so."

"Please."

He stopped the truck. The clutch was giving out; they settled, lurching. She smiled at him and took the bike and waved and pedaled off.

He was not sorry. He started up and turned at the fork and made for Nickerson's. She'd known enough, he knew, not to bring some stranger back and maybe knew enough to work the sweat and dust up on her trip's last leg—arriving breathy, cheerful, just in time for supper and not admitting how she'd lost her way or found it, giving a fair imitation of hunger and hungry enough anyhow to do justice to the soup . . .

But it was as though his lover had returned to him, corporeal. Beth Sieverdsen would enter rooms as though she knew he'd rise, expectant, and would walk to a room's door as though she knew beforehand that some man would sweep it open. She had accepted compliments as he'd seen men take insults—as though it were the rightful portion, properly bestowed. Praise had been her rightful portion from the start.

He could not return to teaching or abide the noise of campus, but Ballard spent long hours in the library in town. Now scholarship—the habit of research and fact-based speculation—compelled him once again. There was a local family whose history at first engaged and then, little by little, engrossed him. The Newcomb family was well established and well documented; they had arrived in Catamount in 1720, traveling inland from Maine.

To begin with they were trappers and farmers and then timber barons and bankers and legislators and railroad owners, among the magnates of the region. In the nineteenth century they caused to be constructed a mansion on the hill that now housed the Historical Society. One Newcomb was elected governor of Vermont and served for two terms with distinction, though he died in the Hoosac Inn in bed with the landlord's daughter. The manner of his dying—a heart attack, suggested some, a pistol-whipping, others said—became his claim to fame. They wrote a song about him: *Pretty Polly, lock the door*.

Then family fortunes declined. During the Revolutionary War they had fought at Ethan Allen's side; in the Civil War they furnished a whole company with uniforms and ammunition and blankets. In the Spanish Civil War the brother of the present patriarch was killed, while distributing guns for the Lincoln Brigade, and his father died in the Ardèche. In Vietnam the last surviving grandson lost a leg, and he returned from Phnom Penh with a horror of bright light and mosquitoes and any sort of sudden noise or intersecting cross street or path with a dark turning. His name was Jason Newcomb and he rolled up and down the length of Park Hill in his wheelchair, obsessively patrolling the north side of the street. Jason played a pennywhistle: *Pretty Polly, lock the door. Pretty Polly went to war.*

An uncle that he barely knew—a shoe manufacturer in St. Louis—left Ballard a small legacy, and the sum augmented his disability insurance. With this new income he hired a housekeeper, Dorothy LaCosta, who came to work three times a week. "Just call me Dot," she said. "But you, you're the professor. You wouldn't like me saying, *Paul*. Admit it, Professor," she said.

Dot shopped and cooked and cleaned those rooms he chose to occupy, straightening his papers and polishing his desk; she brought her own lunch in a brown paper bag and wore slippers while she worked. Retired from her job as assistant postmistress in East Arlington, she was lean and sallow and disapproving, and muttered as she pushed the vacuum cleaner back and forth across the faded rugs or mopped the kitchen floor. Her face was deeply wrinkled, cross-hatched, as though she had been plump when young, and she sucked on her teeth while he paid her, then drove off in her Plymouth with an air of injured honesty. Dot had a grandson with a stamp collection, and she liked to sort and cut the stamps off Ballard's foreign mail. She was, she told him, born again, and she could not understand why he wasn't a believer and why he wouldn't come with her to church. It won't hurt a hair of your head, she assured him every Thursday, leaving, and you'd feel much better if you let yourself be comforted by the goodness of Our Lord. If you just for one single minute accepted Him into your heart. Don't be so snooty, Professor, don't let yourself think for one single minute there's no salvation on earth.

Dot's efforts at conversion had no effect on Ballard; he only half-heard her, half-watched. He practiced his guitar. He listened to Segovia and John Williams and Julian Bream. For work was his therapy, work was his comfort, work was his way in the world. And with increasing frequency while reading or taking notes or writing he felt what he would have called pleasure—the dawning conviction and half-available half-certainty that things indeed made sense.

Ballard saw in the Newcombs' declension a syntax of New England, its rise and period of national and transatlantic power and quasi-comic scandals and then its slow collapse. There was a system, a coherent pattern to recurrence, and it seemed imperative to chart that pattern: synchronic, diachronic (as with a sine curve, a sound wave), the past and present fused. *Pretty Polly lock the door, Pretty Polly kiss me more.* For there was also entropy, and the family in decline provided an example of what he long before described, in his article on Grandma Moses, as the unmediated version of the barn and farmyard: dust to ashes, ash to dust.

His new book was titled *Still Life, With Apples*, and there were illustrations (daguerreotypes, quilt patterns, wartime requisition orders, photographs and death masks) interspersed. This narrative analysis of the Newcomb family, its changing presence in the town, appeared in 1991 and proved a large success. Lavishly, reviewers praised him and were reminded of his excellence and previous achievement in the field.

Paul Ballard, they declared, is the rarest of creatures, a public philosopher, and his clear-eyed history merits respectful attention. No one else now writing has a firmer grasp on simultaneity, the presence of the past. Here at last is a dialectician competent to deal—and one who does so in a fashion mercifully free of jargon—with the problem posed.

In this ground-breaking study of Professor Ballard's we may see the relation of object as subject and vice versa, as well as the objective and subjective nature of reality: how the "objective" may be viewed as a sum of subjectivities. Memory and landscape have long been this author's twin preoccupations, and the conjunction of the two requires both an intellectual rigor and a wide-ranging erudite wit.

"Paul Ballard?"

"Yes."

"Paul?"

"Speaking."

"I can't believe it."

"What?"

"That I got through to you."

"It's not that difficult," he said.

"Oh, yes it is."

"You have the advantage," he said. "You know who you're speaking to but I don't know who's called."

"I'm sorry. I did try to write."

"Excuse me, please. Who's calling?"

"This is *the* Paul Ballard? The one who wrote *Musical Silence*?"

"Yes."

"The one who went to school at Yale? The one who shaved his moustache in, say, 1969? The one with the mole on his right upper thigh? Who can't remember me."

And then he did remember. "Christ," he said.

"How *are* you, Paul?"

"I know your voice."

"I thought you might." After a moment Elizabeth asked: "*Esse est percipii*. Do you remember that? It's Bishop Berkeley's dictum: 'To exist is to perceive.'"

"And?"

"I do exist," she said. There was static on the phone. "And it's a local call."

"Excuse me?"

"I'm staying at the Paradise Motel. And I need you to drive over here; I do have news. We do."

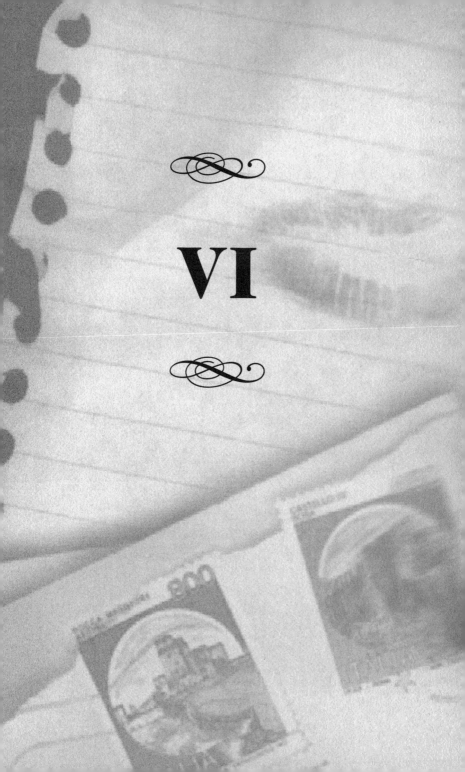

VI

T‍HE PARADISE MOTEL was set back from Cottage Street, perched on a hill. It had a courtyard and a swimming pool and view of the Green Mountains, and it was painted green. The courtyard itself framed three sides of a square, with an office at the south-facing side, and a two-story structure to the north. A Coca-Cola dispensing machine and a red telephone booth flanked the office entryway; there was a coffee shop and a laundry truck idling beyond it, and a flagpole by the office with an American flag. The lights of the *Vacancy* sign flickered fitfully: on, off, on again.

Ballard idled through the parking lot, looking for Room 43. The motel was clapboard, dingy, and the paint on its shutters had peeled. Only a few cars remained in the lot, and Elizabeth's—so she had told him on the phone—was a rented light-blue Chevrolet; he found it and pulled up.

There was linen on the walkway outside Room 43. The curtains had been drawn, the blinds were down. A woman with a broom and mop pushed a service trolley down the arcade of doors to his left. A boy and girl ran from the kiddy-pool while Ballard watched, white bathroom towels around their necks like collars, and he studied the shape of the clouds. *Nimbus*, he told himself, *cumulus, cirrus*, but could not recall which was which.

It was one o'clock. Trucks downshifted loudly on the steep slope of Cottage Street, and he listened to the radio the cleaning woman carried with her on the cart. There were trumpets, violins. There was a tub of pink geraniums, and a vine he could not recognize festooning the kiddy-pool fence. Trying to calm himself, waiting, he stared at the motel. The light slanted softly, cloud-diffused, and he removed his dark glasses and pictured himself at the door to Elizabeth's room, knocking on it, watching the peephole, waiting for an instant till the white door would open and she would stand there smiling and then, softly, step aside . . .

It did not work that way. He could not leave the car. Her voice had echoed on the phone as though from a great distance, and he wished he had not answered or that she had not called. Ballard bent towards the steering wheel and rested his forehead there, stunned. There was nothing she could offer him he wanted to accept and nothing he could offer that she might find useful. He closed his eyes and counted to two hundred, ascending by twos; then he reversed the procedure, subtracting. When Elizabeth knocked on the passenger window and he raised his head again to see an aging stranger peering in at him her face was blurred and various and he was frightened of it, fearful, and there were, he knew, tears in his eyes.

"Is it you, Paul?"

"Yes."

"It's you. It's really, *really* you."

He nodded.

"I wasn't sure you'd come."

"I wasn't either."

"Well, hello."

"You look"—he tried to remember the way people talk—"wonderful."

"Come in, if you'd like to. There's coffee. Or"—she pointed down the parking lot—"a coffee shop."

He opened the car door.

"Have you had lunch?"

"No."

"I was watching from the window. I saw you driving up, and then I saw you park."

He stood. He closed the door.

"Are you all right?"

Pain flared in his right knee, then faded. He wondered, should he kiss her cheek? Pain punched his hip.

"We've changed," said Elizabeth. "I wasn't sure . . ."

"I wasn't expecting . . ."

"We're old people now."

"I am," he said. "Not you."

"I'm glad you came."

"I couldn't not . . ." He spread his hands, then clasped them.

"It's a terrible motel, the 'Paradise.' It's hell."

"I'm sorry."

"Yes. Well, purgatory maybe."

"Did I keep you waiting long?"

"Not very long." She smiled. "A quarter of a century."

All such banter was beyond him; he made no answer and—while the light careened madly from office to phone booth to coffee shop to swimming pool—walked into Room 43.

The wallpaper was green. The room had a beige carpet and an armchair and a bureau with a television on it, and a mirror opposite the bed. The bed remained unmade. She had been unable to sleep. The ceiling plasterboard was cracked; she had examined the pattern of what were no doubt supposed to be climbing roses and a picket fence on the wallpaper, with a bluebird or blackbird or robin perched at the edge of the fence. Air blew noisily from the heating and cooling unit underneath the window, and beige curtains billowed in the created wind.

Her suitcase lay athwart the coffee table, and there were *Elle* and the *Economist* by the side of the bed, and a copy of the *Catamount Clarion* open on the floor. She had attempted to read it for much of the morning, trying to make sense of the local real-estate ads and the movie schedules and the question of the landfill and who was responsible for and should be assessed the charges pertaining to the proposed cleanup of toxic wastes from the car-battery plant that had gone bankrupt and closed down in 1992, but could not concentrate. Twice she had showered and twice dried her hair. There were school board elections and budgets and a profile of the man in Shaftsbury who qualified for the Olympics in the triathlon. There would be an auction for cars.

Paul Ballard sat. The armchair had, she noticed now, a headrest; he leaned against it gingerly and then sat forward again. He settled his hands on his knees. The first shock of seeing him faded, and the gray hair and lined face and slack posture and stomach fused with the shape of the man she remembered, as though her vision blurred then cleared in a kind of doubling focus. Elizabeth shut her right eye, then the left, and his image leaped forward then back.

There were so many things to tell him she barely knew where to begin. She wanted to tell him how strange it all seemed to be sitting together in Catamount now, to be adults together inside a motel and after all these years. Her daughter Serena was moving to Charleston for the summer and had been offered a job there in the Historical Society, a Conservation Internship, nonpaying naturally, but it was what Serena hoped to do professionally later on, and she expected her mother to help find an apartment and help her move in. So Elizabeth agreed to come and was passing through Vermont, had flown to Boston from Milan and thought she should—what was the word?—acclimatize herself, getting over the time change and what deep-sea divers call the bends and therefore start here in the north and drive slowly south. She understood, of course, it was a peculiar way to travel, not the wrong but long way to South Carolina, since she could have flown straight to Atlanta, but she wasn't used to driving and she needed to get ready and in any case, she admitted, Serena wasn't really waiting, was ready to wait, and her son Bill would join them both in St. Simon's or St. Catherine's or one of those Georgia Sea Islands where everybody goes these days, or is it Hilton Head?

Where are you going? he did not ask.

I don't know, she did not say.

The family place up in northern Michigan had been burned, she learned, in March. Her parents were dead—did he know that?—her father dying early on and her mother just two years ago, of not exactly a heart attack but something similar, exhaustion, a kind of systemic collapse; her second husband had been a devoted golfer so they moved to a retirement community called Sun City in Arizona and played golf all day, every day, rain or shine except it never rained. One morning on the fifteenth hole she simply lay down on the green and tried once but failed to get up; her mother gave up the ghost, they said, with a smile on her face and everybody said it must have been painless, a blessing, she was doing what she loved to do and had been preparing to putt. So Elizabeth inherited the camp in Hessel, and it had been her intention to return there every summer, but then the house burned down. No one was hurt, thank goodness, and in some sense they'd been lucky since it wasn't totally destroyed because of the volunteer

fireman who happened to be passing by and called in
the alarm. She herself had a suspicion that maybe it was
arson (strange, isn't it, or didn't Paul think so, that a
fireman should be driving by, out there in the middle of
nowhere, in the middle of the winter in the middle of the
week) and therefore the blaze had maybe been not carelessness on the part of some ice fisherman whose attention wandered, but something a good deal more
suspicious, a good deal more predictable in the context
of—what was the word?—pyromania. Elizabeth just
couldn't bear to see the place in ruins, blackened beams,
bare ruined floors, she'd seen the photographs, with the
second-story windows broken and the roof caved in,
and couldn't bring herself to go out there, not yet. But
her son Bill had no such anxiety; he was flying on to
Hessel soon and would find out what had happened and
was ready to hire the carpenters or do the job himself:
six-foot-two and counting, he was just so *competent*. His
idea of a summer vacation was to take a backpack and a
pair of walking shoes, with maybe an ice axe or hammer
and a bathing suit and sleeping bag and say "See ya,
Mom." Serena, *evidammente*, was altogether different,
was hanging out in Evanston, manicuring her fingernails and sailing with her boyfriend who would get an
MBA. Did Paul remember that she had two children
and one almost-ex-husband called Michael who was
staying in Cortona with a man he had lived with in
Rome?

Elizabeth said none of this. She poured him cold coffee instead. "It isn't any good," she said. "The coffee."

"Fine. It's fine."

"What you see is what you get," she said.

"How *are* you?"

"Fine, I'm fine."

Again there was silence between them. It's like, she tried to say, a dream, it's how we talk out loud in dreams but everything stays silent nevertheless. She sipped at her Styrofoam cup and the brown tasteless powdered water; the heating unit hummed. But she needed to tell him the rest of her story, the way it had felt taking off from Linate, and how she brought along her magazines and doused herself with perfume and put on a proper dress of the sort that people used to fly in when airplanes were not so much the rule as the exception, because the airport nowadays is more like a bus station than what it used to be, remember, a bastion of power and white executive privilege. Had he noticed? did he travel much? had he seen all those families in shorts and straw hats and T-shirts with slogans or embroidered pineapples, with portable radios blaring?

Elizabeth heard herself sounding, she knew, like just the kind of person she had wanted to eliminate or at least indoctrinate when she was young, when twenty-one, a person like her mother or her mother's bridge friends or her father's golf partners and right-wing impossible Republican business associates, who had patronized her all through childhood, who disregarded or pinched her. But nonetheless there *was* some value—she had to admit it, she had to be fair—in the ancient proprietary impulse and zealous bourgeois hoarding, some essential paradox at the heart of democracy or at least our version of contemporary capitalism: the more popu-

lar the resort or museum and universal its access (be it
airport, museum, or beach or hotel) the less she desired
to go.

Therefore in fact the true conservative might *not*
build a hotel and *not* develop a shoreline and *not* allow
a price war or cut-rate no-frills airport and airline,
and in the grip of this perception—so very much the
sort of thing she used to think, long years before and
courtesy of, who was it, Huey Newton, Bobby Seale?
before she had become neither a solution to the problem nor a part of it but someone entirely *elsewhere*, absent—she very much had needed to inoculate herself
with wine, since trip by trip she felt increasingly not
decreasingly frightened of flying. And strange that she
should feel this way, since after all she'd crisscrossed
the Atlantic more times than she would care to count,
had come home every summer, or nearly, though not
to New England, and did still think of it as home, still
wanted to be an American, and never more so, paradoxically, than when most entirely Italian-seeming:
pawing through the mounded *vonghole* or artichokes or
cooking pears, disputing with the pharmacist or making conversation with the postman—but needed to
come back again, to visit cold Lake Michigan and the
warm Sea Islands and even their shared refuge now,
the Paradise Motel.

Elizabeth said none of this. Like the old man he was
Paul Ballard sniffed; he blew his nose. She watched him
watch the wall. He sipped at his coffee, not swallowing
it. She could find nothing to say.

"What brings you here?" he asked at last.

"Brings me?"

"Well, what have you been up to? What have you been doing?"

"Doing?"

"I'm sorry, I don't seem to know what to ask."

"You've stayed here in Catamount? Teaching?"

"I've stayed here. Not teaching," he said.

"Did you ever marry?"

"No."

"Are you . . . together with someone?"

He shook his head.

"But you stayed in that house? All this time?"

"I live alone," he said.

"Oh."

The clock by her bedside was also a radio. It had red digits; she watched three 1's at once, and then the right-hand number moved; she read 1:12.

"You called me," Ballard pointed out. "You did say you wanted to talk."

"I did," she admitted.

He sat back; he folded his hands.

"But let's not discuss it, okay?" She watched the clock. "Not right away, I mean. Let's have some other conversation."

"About?"

"The things we used to talk about . . ."

Ballard made a movement of impatience. "What should be our subject: the weather?"

Now Elizabeth felt condescended to again, goaded again, and so she blurted out what she had planned so carefully, prepared to say so cautiously: "We had a child."

He stared at her.

"A baby."

"Had?"

"Have," she said. "We have a child."

"Where?"

"Here. I just found out."

"Here?" he repeated. Involuntarily, he scanned the room. "Where?"

"A daughter. She's living in Vermont."

And this was true. This was her long slow recurrent nightmare that could not be dismissed as dream; this was her haunted daylit reverie: the letter from someone called Sally Axelrod who had tracked her down. It had been typed, on blue paper, and the envelope said "Please forward," and was doubly secured with Scotch tape. "Dear Elizabeth," the letter began. There were four pages, single-spaced, and the signature was also typed and there had been no date. The return address was a post office box in Burlington, Vermont.

On the day of her twenty-first birthday—so Sally

wrote—she had asked her parents for the facts of her adoption. She herself had known too little of the story, and one of the things that this letter might do is maybe change all that, because she wanted to set an example and tell everything she knew. She had always understood, of course, that she had been adopted, and was legally entitled to the facts of her own history and on her twenty-first birthday declared that it's time to name names. They had been sitting at breakfast, she wrote, and spending the weekend together in a way that didn't happen much except on birthdays or holidays now, because she had grown bored with the family place in Vermont. She had attended NYU and majored there in Social Sciences, though mostly what she did was hang around the film school and hang out with her friends; they'd been working on a screenplay about a fashion photographer who was adopted and sleeps with a business executive who turns out to be her father, although she doesn't know this, and the man's wife, her mother, who actually runs the ad agency, dies in a car crash at the crossroads and so she marries the guy.

Then all sorts of complicated hell breaks loose, because it's a contemporary version of the Oedipus story, from a feminist perspective, and all about child abuse and incest and how even good intentions can prove catastrophic. So one bright morning Sally woke up and decided it was time to learn about her own personal history; she didn't mean, she meant, that she had memories of abuse or anything like that about her own particular childhood, only it became important to find out.

So she had asked her parents over orange juice and

chain-link sausages and pancakes: what can you tell me, folks? Her mother didn't want to talk, she said let's let bygones be bygones, let's leave well enough alone. But Dad took *her* side, he often did, and while he was pouring the syrup and cutting up his stack of pancakes said if Sally wants to know we have no right to hide the truth, she has the right to her personal history if she decides to own it. Let's let sleeping dogs lie, urged her mother again, but agreed to fetch the file.

The folder wasn't very thick, although years ago her dad had tried—not very hard, he admitted—to find out information about both of the birth parents in this case. He himself had been an investigative journalist and knew the way to track down facts, but only uncovered the mother. While they were washing dishes—she washed them while he dried, it was their father-and-daughter ritual, their way of spending time together in the kitchen—he said her biological mother was American and had been raised in Grosse Pointe Shores but had signed release forms in November 1970 and, if she was still alive, was living somewhere in Italy and gave her Elizabeth's name.

That had been four years ago. To begin with she did nothing, only carried the file everywhere as if it were a substitute for certainty and thought well if I *need* to, if I *want* to, if I *decide* it's important I can always get in touch. It had been up to her, she wrote, to choose which way to go. And so she had written this letter—taking her own sweet time doing it, keeping it around with her for weeks and months, from place to place, from job to job, adding and subtracting and wondering if she should even bother to send it—not so much as a result of but as part of the process of decision making; she was trying to establish if she really did hope to make contact and wanted full disclosure. Then this past winter up in Sugarbush she'd hurt her knee and had to have an operation and decided to recuperate not in New York but Sandgate, since the house was empty. She was working on subscription lists for a radio station in Rutland, and had a lot of time to think, the job was undemanding, not exactly MTV, she was lying around eating bon-bons and her parents came on weekends so they hung out together. Sally was twenty-five by now and wanted to be clear about this: she wanted nothing, she needed nothing from a stranger in Italy called Sieverdsen-Vire. Except a few plain answers and a little human clarity. And that was the reason she wrote.

I'm five foot eight, wrote Sally, I'm blond and have blue eyes; is it the way you looked? Used to look? Still do? My left leg is half an inch short. I'm all right without you, she wrote, I'm perfectly healthy, I'm fine.

But I do guess I want to know if this was your idea and how well you knew my father and if he himself was part of the decision-making process way back when. Is he alive? A person doesn't disappear, she wrote, or maybe you were Catholic or maybe too young or ashamed; but would you mind explaining it, would you tell me who you are and where you are and what you do and if I have brothers and sisters and just what you were thinking and here's your big chance Mom. Your chance of a lifetime: write back.

"I don't," Ballard breathed, "believe this."

"Why not?"

"Why should I? How *can* I?"

"Paul, I wouldn't lie to you."

"No." The ceiling fixture flickered. He looked at it, then her. "You never did."

"That hasn't changed."

"It hasn't?"

"No."

"Well, what's her name?"

"Sally."

"Our daughter?"

"Yes. Our daughter, Sally Axelrod. Tell the truth, you didn't know?"

"I didn't, no."

"Or even guess?"

He shook his head.

"I thought you guessed it anyhow. I think that's what made me so angry."

"Angry?"

She nodded.

"Well, have you met her?"

"No. I'm planning to. We've been writing back and forth, and when I got to this country I called."

"Does she expect you?"

"It's the reason I came."

He asked their daughter's name again; Elizabeth repeated it. He asked her once more, was she sure? She said, yes, Axelrod.

There was a brown oblong stain on the wallpaper; there had been water damage. Paul Ballard shut his eyes. Reaching out he touched the wall and, leaning, put weight on his hand. Like a kaleidoscope he twisted—even as he shook his head, even as he turned from his companion in the dingy room—the pattern of his past was rearranged. Like magnetic filings on a metal disc his history now changed.

She positioned herself at the door to his house, the road dust on her clothes and face, and he answered unwillingly, brusquely. Her name was Sally Axelrod; she said so when he asked. When salesmen knocked—or census takers, or students soliciting donations for Greenpeace or the Kiwanis Club Christmas Drive or Jehovah's Witnesses or candidates for senator—Ballard sent them packing, always. But this one had been different somehow: self-contained, incurious, and he offered her a glass of water and a ride.

"I couldn't do that," Sally said.

"Why not?"

"It's too much trouble."

"Going that way anyway . . ."

He could picture her Schwinn bicycle and how he'd jumped down off the porch and slung it on the burlap in his pickup bed. He remembered how he'd let her out not two miles from Sandgate and the place she told him she stayed for the summer and how she lived in Manhattan and had gone out exploring for the morning and, without street signs, was lost. He had known the name already: Axelrod. But it meant little at the time, carried only a faint echo, and if he noticed it at all had noticed it only as coincidence, a name not so uncommon as to invoke father and daughter but perhaps some distant relative called Axelrod or perhaps nothing at all. The girl pedaled off, not looking back, and even now, remembering, he thought surely her arrival must have been an accident and not intention veiled.

"My mother would be angry."

"Why?" Ballard asked.

"Because of the trouble I'm being . . ."

"No trouble."

"But she'd be angry anyhow. At me making you come all the way . . ."

Nor had he then connected her with the man in the grocery store, the BMW outside with bicycles on the roof rack a decade before. This too he recollected with a selective clarity—the check-out line, the wedge of cheese, the Agway cap Axelrod wore. But the reporter had been pumping him for knowledge, testing him in Harrington's (the flash philosopher subsiding already to yokel, the city sophisticate transformed by time to this forgetful bump-kin with a backpack), not asking for an interview or quote. With his flattery of Ballard's books and the suggestion that they talk about the sixties, with his pretense of uncertainty as to Beth Sieverdsen's name he had offered a gambit: refused.

And satisfied perhaps with the teacher's mute intransigence, satisfied there'd be no claim forthcoming from that quarter Sam Axelrod had left and told his wife there's nothing new, no news in his part of the world. Or perhaps the journalist decided, on the principle of conscious inattention, that what he didn't know for sure could surely cause no harm. "Let's just forget it, okay?" he would say, and his wife would have answered, "Okay."

Ballard parted the curtains; he stood staring out. In his head language unreeled. He had a child; they had a child; I have a daughter; we have a daughter, he wanted to say. He could barely make sense of the phrase and repeated it: we have a daughter, we do. The words were a refrain, a conjugation in a foreign tongue but one that he could not complete. She has a child; he has a child; they have a child; we have a child, he told himself, I have a daughter too.

"She wrote you?"

"Yes. And I wrote back. And then when I arrived I called . . ."

"What did she sound like?"

"Sound like?"

"Was she, oh, articulate? I mean, did she make sense to you?"

Elizabeth stood.

"Why did she write?" Ballard asked.

"To establish some sort of connection. To make what she called 'contact.' To find out what happened."

"What happened?"

"Is it so very strange, Paul? So wrong of her? Would you call it, what *would* you call it, 'inappropriate'?"

"After all these years?"

"Yes."

"For no apparent reason? With no apparent motive?"

"Let's not begin again," she said.

Outside, it was starting to rain. "Begin what?"

"Let's not start arguing, okay? I mean, I only just arrived here. She only just wrote."

The boy and girl he had seen in the pool were with their parents now: dressed, loading duffel bags into a trunk.

"Should we go there together?" asked Ballard. "Is that what you want from me?"

"Yes."

The boy slammed the car door. He rolled down the window. His sister leaned out of it, waving. The family drove off.

But what had she expected, Elizabeth asked herself, pulling open the closet door, hunting her raincoat; what had she hoped she might find? Not, surely, the companion of her own long-vanished youth. She stepped into the warm wet air and handed Ballard the room key: 43. Its brown plastic key tag was cracked.

With a formal caution he unlocked the passenger side of the car and waited while she sat and strapped herself into the seat and then closed the door again and he opened his own door and started the engine and turned on the wipers. Next he pulled out a pocket handkerchief and made meticulous crescents in the mist inside the window.

"All right," he offered. "I'll take us to Sandgate. Let's go."

"How far is it?"

"Not far," he said, "a half an hour maybe. Northeast."

For some time they rode in silence. Ballard focused on his driving—down Cottage Street and North Street and then Main Street and north on Route 7—while Elizabeth allowed herself to drift, and the image of her family's burned "camp" in Michigan appeared to her once more. There were fishing rods, canoe paddles and oarlocks and badminton rackets and snowshoes; in the high heat, they fused. The cedar shingles, open beams and high sloping roof and wooden porch ignited. She had been told, she reminded herself, that damage to the structure was extensive but not total; it had been caught in time. Much of the house had been saved.

Yet when she tried to see it she saw everything as wreckage: the rooms she'd been a child in, and later brought her children to, the pine trees and the wooden dock from which she'd first, at eleven, sighted an eagle, the rocking chair and kitchen counter and stairwell and pillows and mounted stag's head, the wedding photographs and folded flag and calendar provided yearly with the compliments of the Search Bay Real Estate and Insurance Agency, the beds and card tables and hooked rugs and cracked leather ottoman were, when she shut her eyes, burning. A Ping-Pong table buckled, snapped and popped. A watercolor of the woods—the first she'd painted, then given her parents for Christmas—melted in its frame. Glass crashed. The salad bowls and pewter mugs and baseball gloves and almanacs and reproductions of John James Audubon's shorebirds and wicker basket with Scrabble and Monopoly and Clue, the dried floral arrangements on the mantel, the cans in the pantry, the boots and slickers in the hall: all these were ruined too.

Her son would fix it. Her son would arrive. Her son would take care of things, surely. Bill was full of plans and hopefulness, his tool belt on his narrow waist, his bandanna at his neck. Therefore she turned her head again and what she saw was elsewhere, not in this car but open air; she was watching what would happen with her son in Michigan this summer while he rebuilt the house. He had asked if he could do it; he said he needed practice and it *matters* to me, Mom.

Elizabeth had an idea—a conviction so strong she could taste it—that Bill would meet his first girlfriend while in the Hessel lumber store, while pricing pine, and now the house was fading, fading, and what she focused on instead was her wide-shouldered boy and a girl hand in hand, walking the beach, wearing denim jackets, sharing a soda or maybe a beer. The beach was backlit, a stage set, streaked gauzily with mist and foam, so where they walked was nowhere actual and she had the feeling—no, the certainty, she told herself—that if she reached to touch them they would prove only air . . .

She wished her children well. She loved them very much. But they no longer needed scrutiny or her premonitory supervision; they fled from her as once to Rome and traveled on alone. Serena, the older, would marry, and her present half-feigned interest in the Charleston project would elide into antiques; her house would acquire objects as though by magnetic attraction, as if by collective volition, the marriage of old wood with wood, old carvings with gold leaf. The dining room and library would accumulate sideboys and pewter and portraits and highboys and corner cupboards and ancient kitchen implements, and she would take it on herself to catalogue the contents of the silver chest . . .

Elizabeth, she told herself, was done with that part of the job. She had watched over Bill and Serena until the act of watching seemed, if not precisely pointless, at least besides the point; she could shut her eyes and *see* them with no effort at two months old, two years old, twelve. In her head she carried a photo album always: *Serena on the swingset, Bill at the beach. Bill blowing out candles, Serena in her tutu, being coy. Serena in the family canoe, holding up a paddle, the water dripping in a kind of permanent transience captured by Kodachrome, Bill with his gutted six-pound bass, his gun . . .*

And therefore she tried not to cry. It was her first child, the stranger, she needed to see. *I will not*, Elizabeth told herself, crying, *I won't, I won't.* She stared out the window while Ballard inched forward in an intersection, his directional signal on, his windshield wipers slapping. What had she planned to find in him, or he in her, that would restore or remedy the past?

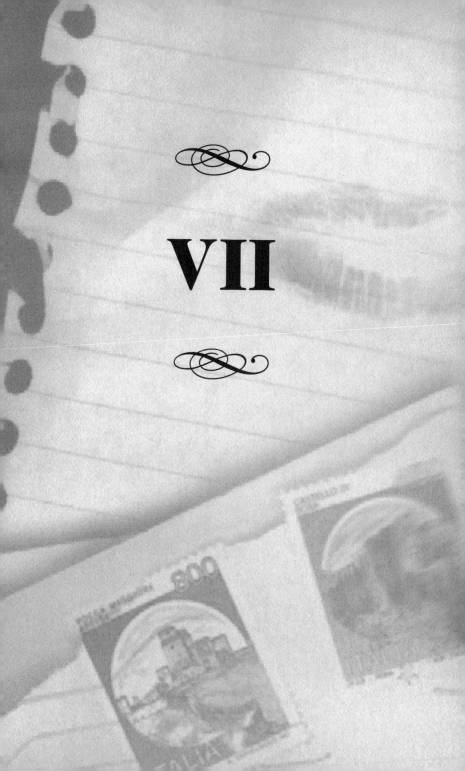

VII

SANDGATE CONSISTED OF a crossroads, a village green and church. A grange hall stood next to a grocery store and four white clapboard houses faced south, each with white brick chimneys and red-and-black patterned slate roofs. There was a cemetery behind a picket fence and what might have been a bandstand in the center of the green. A flagpole with an American flag and a flowerbed with pansies and petunias rimmed the bandstand's base.

The rain had stopped. They asked directions of a man with a weed whacker, who pointed away from Main Street. "Can't miss it," he told them. "First turn on your left."

The Axelrod house was set back from the road, behind a low stone wall. It too was of painted white clapboard, with green shutters and a weather vane, and there were elaborate plantings by the trellised kitchen door. Prosperity seemed palpable in the curve of the brick walkway and the hosta and impatiens by the path. There was a circular drive of white gravel, and a black Range Rover, freshly washed, stood gleaming by the garage.

"We're here." Elizabeth pulled down the visor and stared at the vanity mirror. "Don't be nervous. Are you nervous?"

"No."

"Well, *I* am. Christ, I'm nervous." She traced her lips with lipstick, pursed and blotted them, and then added blush to her cheeks. "We don't have to do this— together, I mean. She's not expecting you."

"No?"

"Don't be offended. I couldn't be certain."

"Of what?"

"That you would want to come with me. To come and meet Sally, I mean. Or even if we'd meet at all."

"Why?"

"Listen to you, only *listen* to you." She touched his coat sleeve lightly and then withdrew her hand.

"What?"

"Please don't go all Vermontish and monosyllabic on me, Paul. You *used* to talk in sentences . . ."

"That's true," he said. "I did."

She unbuckled her seat belt, then stood. Irresolute, he too emerged, then rolled up the passenger window and followed where she led. The green door opened inward and, from his vantage point, three feet behind, it was as though Ballard saw double: the woman who stood in the doorway was the woman he'd seen twenty-five years earlier, her absolute and mirror image, the mother of his daughter who was in fact his child.

"Hello."

"Hello."

"You must be Sally."

"Yes."

"I'm Elizabeth Sieverdsen." She held out her hand. "Sieverdsen-Vire."

"Hello."

"And this is Paul Ballard."

"We've met before," he ventured.

"We have?"

"I think so, yes."

"When?" She did not look at him; she was staring at Elizabeth.

"You were a whole lot younger then."

"I don't remember. I'm sorry."

"It doesn't matter," Ballard said. "You were riding your bike, remember?"

"My parents"—perceptibly, she stressed the word— "are in Woodstock. There's a wedding there."

"May we come in?" Elizabeth asked.

As though on a model's ramp, turning, Sally Axelrod swiveled and walked back inside. The two of them followed, then stood in the entryway, on the slate floor. She took their raincoats and hung them on pegs in the white-walled mudroom and ushered them into the kitchen.

"Did you have trouble finding us?"

"Not really, no."

"The house, I mean . . ."

"I've practiced this a thousand times," Elizabeth declared, her voice high-pitched. "I simply don't know how to start."

"Where did you practice? How?"

"Oh, everywhere. In Italy, on the plane, the whole way driving. Yesterday, when you answered the phone, when I called you to say I was coming. I did try to prepare for this . . ."

They were standing in the kitchen: a country kitchen out of *Yankee* magazine. There were implements from the colonial period: wooden bellows, candle molds. There were cut flowers and dried flowers and a wreath of bay leaves and cast-iron skillets hanging from a wooden beam. "My parents are in Woodstock," Sally said again. "A wedding . . ."

"Do they come here often?" Ballard asked.

"Not really, no. For long weekends, sometimes. And the month of August."

"And you?" asked Elizabeth.

"I wrote you about that, remember?" She was her mother's height exactly and she had her mother's hair before time darkened it. She moved with the same long-legged grace and had her mother's coloring and her father's eyes.

"I remember. Is it better now? Your knee, I mean."

"Is he the teacher?" Sally asked.

"Who?"

For the first time she turned to Ballard. "You."

"I was."

"I thought so."

"Who told you?"

"Sam. When you drove me home that day, he said you were a teacher. At Catamount College."

"So you *do* remember . . ."

She made no answer. The totality of her attention was focused on her mother. "You could have found me if you wanted. If you tried."

"I could have, yes."
"Well, did you try?"
"I didn't," said Elizabeth. "Till now."

Light fell across rose petals in the white stoneware bowl on the oak cutting board, and dust-motes rode the air. In the middle distance there were photographs of Sally: carving pumpkins, on a swing set, on a horse. She was holding a diploma and a bicycle and tennis racket and, when fifteen or so, a guitar. She was standing in a prom dress at the bottom of a staircase; she was lying in a hammock or licking at an ice-cream cone or grinning gap-toothed at the camera and reaching out her hand.

You don't have to answer, Elizabeth said, her speech at first half-audible, but you do need to listen and let me have my say. She had thought about it long enough, had thought of nothing else, and now she had, well, not so much an explanation as a confession to make. She spoke about her ancient house, the olive groves, the walls so thick they positively sweat in summer, the fig tree by the window of the room she lay in by herself at nighttime and the pattern of the fig leaves on the ceiling, how they moved. Elizabeth described the way it felt to leave Cortona, to have discovered in her forties that domestic life was finished and her husband had no use for her and her children too were gone. *Il postino* arrives every morning, she said, and he brings me nothing important, a bill for this, a bill for that, or maybe an announcement from a gallery in Rome. Or a postcard from a distant friend or a year-end informational letter from relatives I wouldn't recognize, saying Tom has gone to college and Dick has earned a promotion and Harry's recovering nicely, thank you, from back surgery. Then one fine day he brings me *you* . . .

The kitchen clock struck the hour; a cuckoo emerged, bleating "Cuckoo" three times. Elizabeth had heard, she said, about a woman who woke up one day with the conviction she should change her life and be of service to others. This happened in Sarasota, or Palm Beach, or maybe Saratoga Springs—one of those upper-class enclaves where the wealthy retire to die. This particular divorcée was fifty, or maybe fifty-five. According to the story, the vision had come to the woman at night, in what she supposed was a dream state: herself with bandages and medicine, with smiling children on her lap and bowls of soup bubbling on stoves. Her life until that moment had been self-centered, egotistical, a prosperous and wholly familiar arrangement of houses and warm coats and cars.

On the morning in question, however, the lady woke up filled with charitable resolve. She would change everything, she knew, and redefine her way of being in the world. So she made the necessary inquiries and identified and then contacted an ashram in Calcutta and wrote to say, I'm ready, I want to leave all this behind, I'll come and help you heal the sick and feed the starving and I'll dedicate my energy to helping out the poor.

She sold her house; she invested in stocks; she moved into a friend's apartment and waited for the call.

Seven months later a letter arrived. It was handwritten, and the address had been scrawled. Inside there was the single sentence: *Find your own Calcutta.*

Sally did not interrupt; she leaned against the counter, elbows splayed for balance, and cradled her head in her hands. She sported a Mickey Mouse Swatch on one wrist, silver bracelets on the other, and she appeared attentive. Her blue eyes were wide.

Elizabeth repeated the phrase: *Find your own Calcutta.* Whether this actually happened or not she had no way of knowing, but it was a good story. It was the way she felt that day in Cortona when the letter from Sally arrived. She wasn't suggesting, of course, that Sally was a charitable cause or that she needed saving or required any help. Nor would she herself have tried to make contact; she hated all those articles about birth mothers changing their minds, those surrogates who sued to change the contractual terms by which they'd provided a baby, saying oh no, I don't think so, what's done can be undone. She wasn't suggesting some sort of revisionist history or way of rewriting the past. What's done was entirely done. But as soon as Sally wrote to ask *Who are you, who were you?* she had the right to answer; now that her daughter had made the first move she had the right to respond.

And who she'd been was twenty-one, a kid. Who she'd been was younger then than Sally is this afternoon, and the man she'd made a baby with was no longer part of the picture. We should talk about that too.

He had an accident. We both did, I suppose. Because I never *did* learn, really, what the accident had meant to him or if he'd even *known* that I was pregnant or how he would have reacted and what it would have meant. But what it meant to *me*, she said, was things were over between us, and my own parents were furious and I never really felt I had a choice . . .

In silence while the others watched she fingered the bowl of dried petals. One thing about Vermont, she said, or maybe only this particular part of it: it's a place time passes by. Sandgate looks just the way it looked, I bet, a hundred years ago, there's no population explosion in the Green Mountains anyhow, no strip mining or strip mall. Then, faltering, she spoke about how strange it felt to be back here near Catamount, the town where she had gone to school and one way or another had avoided ever since. It's what you used to like to call—at last she turned to Ballard—irrelevance preserved.

He spread his hands. He nodded. Well anyway, she said, I haven't seen *you* since the day you were born and I haven't been in this part of the world since 1970. If I left Catamount, I told myself, and then the state and then the country, and if I married someone else and started paying taxes and became a proper citizen, a grown-up, I thought I could leave you alone. Yes, Sally, I got pregnant in Vermont. And, yes, I was in school. But you're a grown-up also now, and maybe you can understand what brings me here, what brought me back, and why I'm not alone today and who your actual father is and why I went to Italy. And someday soon I hope you'll meet your sister and your brother, your half-sister and half-brother: Serena, Bill.

What I've been feeling all this time—I don't know a good way to say this, I don't know how else to describe it—is as if I had a shadow self, a second way of being in the world. It's as if the day that I gave birth to you I separated out, and part of me went on with life and part of me just waited. Your father taught philosophy, that used to be his subject. But it isn't really what I mean, not all the stuff about Plato and firelight in caves and being divided from your opposite. What I mean is, Sally, I keep seeing how different it would be if we had stayed together, if I hadn't cut and run. *Find your own Calcutta*: it's time I tried that too.

Outside, there were the sounds of arrival—brakes, an engine shutting off, a car door slammed. There was laughter, then feet across gravel, and then the front door opened and the Axelrods walked in.

"Should we be leaving?" asked Elizabeth.

"Mom, Dad," said Sally. "Hello."

"Hiya, folks," Sam Axelrod offered cozily. He waved from the doorway, not paying attention; he shook himself free from his coat.

"Hello," Paul Ballard said.

"I'm Barbara Axelrod." She handed her husband her own coat and scarf. "I don't believe we've met." Companionably, unconcerned, she nodded at the visitors: two strangers in the kitchen of her house.

"Well, how was the wedding?" asked Sally.

"Fine. Terrific. They asked after you."

"The bride looked beautiful," said Barbara Axelrod. "The whole affair was beautiful." Her hair was jet-black, with a white-dyed plume; she was thin and elegant and rapid in her movements; gold bracelets clanked at her wrist.

"You arranged this, didn't you," said Elizabeth. It was not a question.

Sally shrugged. "I thought they'd be in Woodstock."

"We were." Axelrod emerged from the hallway closet. He had grown portly; his dress shirt was sweat-stained and his black bow tie dangled from the collar. "Drinking Asti Spumante and ducking bouquets."

"Your father did rather too much of the former, dear. I think he thought he was *supposed* to catch that posy. Like the old days back of second base, or maybe playing football, it was—what do you call it?—an interception." Barbara mimed the act of catching. "I had to drive us home."

"Brrroom brroom," said the journalist, as though shifting gears. He did a jig-step, advancing, then put his hand on Sally's arm and smiled at her, proprietary. "I *hate* Asti Spumante. It tastes too damn sweet."

"Elizabeth Vire," said Elizabeth. "Sieverdsen-Vire. I'm glad to meet you, finally."

"Finally?" asked Axelrod. He was wearing a blazer and white flannel pants. He was, it appeared, still half-drunk. "Why finally? Were we supposed to meet before? Hell, any friend of Sally's . . ."

"They're not my friends," said Sally. The hall clock chimed. She looked at the floor, then the wall.

"Are we interrupting something?" Mrs. Axelrod's tone shifted.

"No."

"Something we should know about?"

"Are you sure you came back early?" asked Elizabeth.

"Why?"

"I was wondering," she said. "Just wondering how, how conscious all this, all this *orchestration* must have been. How much you planned it, Sally."

The girl turned away. Irresolute, she switched on the lamp by the bookshelf: there were cookbooks and gardening books.

"We know each other, don't we?" asked the journalist, approaching. "Haven't I seen you here somewhere before?"

"Yes."

"Where? Remind me, pal."

"At Harrington's," Paul Ballard said.

"Harrington's?"

"And then before. When you wrote about Catamount."

"Jesus Christ," said Axelrod. "It's my old pal the professor."

"Correct."

"Hell, it's been years. You never met my wife, now did

you?" Loudly, he performed the introduction. "Barbara, Paul Ballard. It's him."

"Are you proud of yourself, Sally?" Elizabeth asked. "Is this what you wanted?"

"A drink," announced Axelrod. "Hair of the dog." He busied himself at the bar. "What's yours, Professor? Bourbon?"

"No thank you. Not this afternoon."

"You should have seen me, baby"—he focused on Sally again—"doing the end-around. A goddam diving catch it was. I caught that sucker, babycakes. I wanted it for *you*."

"Thanks anyway," said Sally.

"You'd think," declared Axelrod, "this girl doesn't *want* to get married. She's twenty-five and counting and she has more proposals—we used to call them propositions, am I right or am I right?—than you can shake a stick at. Like in the old days, when we were her age." He shook his head. "Christ, the way it used to be . . ."

"Last call, everybody," Barbara said. "My husband needs a nap."

"Don't tell me what I need," he said. "I'll tell you what I *want*. I want to finish this discussion with my old pal Paul Ballard here. And *then* they'll stay for dinner, if there's anything to eat or anybody's hungry . . ."

"No thank you," said Elizabeth.

"*O tempore, or mores*," said Axelrod, surprising them.

"Why did you come here?" Barbara asked. "And why can't you leave us alone?"

Ballard's mind was in a riot of avoidance; he had data to convey. Now that an audience gathered, there was much that he needed to say. There were more people in this room than he was used to talking to, four auditors, eight ears, but he was out of practice and would have to grow accustomed to the complicated back-and-forth of conversation and what, said, remained unsaid . . .

He moved to the window and stood staring out. He wanted to explain, for example, how the idea of gravel courtyards had first been put in service to announce a visitor; in the French château or English manor house a pebble driveway kept a guest or lord or retainer or assassin from arriving with no warning noise. And this was why he'd heard them when they pulled into the driveway and why their arrival, although unexpected, was not in fact or entirely a surprise. He could have told them how the name of this particular crossroads, Sandgate, came from the time that charcoal was a product of the region, how everything they saw and had been driving through was second growth. Did Elizabeth or Sally or anybody in the room believe that the proportion of open land to forested had been reversed within the century, so that what once was open land was now scrub pine and oak; had they heard how, more than a century previous, Daniel Webster spoke to an audience of thousands up on Glastenbury Pass? Did they understand how earlier this crossroads itself was a populous

place?—filled with those who thronged to hear the
silver-tongued and loud-throated orator making his way
across to Manchester—although nothing of that
progress admittedly remained but great burned rotted
hollowed stumps and the occasional rusting logger's
chain or axle and the incoherent wind. He could have
told his daughter how the very road they drove on had
been stone-wall lined, how all of this was pasture once,
how here at least the contemporary process of relentless
construction, road-building and subdivision has been
reversed, for in this nation we have paved over an area
the size of France just to build the interstates, and rarely
may one find a place *less* populous, *less* cheek-by-jowl
than would have been the case a century before. And
even the great Daniel Webster—were he returned by
some time traveler's recurrence or through necromancy
and displacement come to walk these lanes again—
would interrogate the empty air and find no crowd on
Glastenbury Mountain but only the beavers, the squir-
rels, the ghosts . . .

Elizabeth and Sally and the Axelrods paid him no attention. Behind him, people were talking; behind him
they knew what to say. His daughter was repeating that
she hadn't expected this, really, but she wasn't sorry,
really, and somebody was scolding her and somebody
absolving her and someone else was saying that it had to
happen sooner or later anyhow and maybe it makes
sense to talk. But, standing at the window, Ballard emptied out the room once more; the world was a warehouse
of numbers, and he doubled and quadrupled them and
stacked them as though they were apples, a handful, a

bushel, a cartload, a barn. There were debits and credits; things fit. In the room of his reclusiveness there was no distraction, no generations scrabbling at the edges of composure like June bugs at the screens. There's been a fire in my head, Paul Ballard did not say out loud, or, rather, a dull hissing sound, a crepitation only, as of embers and some smoke . . .

He ran his tongue around his lips; he coughed. He cleared his throat. How many times, he asked himself, had he pictured this reunion—in shopping center or meadow or lobby or bed, in city or in countryside, on purpose or by accident; how often had he thought his lover might return? The woman in a passing car or in the elevator of the downtown library while its cream-colored doors closed, ascending, descending, the stranger he believed familiar, the sway of someone's forward stride or shape of their hair or sound of their laughter or tilt of their chin—all these had distracted him often. For years, for decades now he'd dreamed of a reunion or, if not dreamed, imagined what would happen when they met: how Elizabeth would fit within the circle of his arms . . .

"I don't know who arranged this," said Barbara Axelrod, "but it's not a good idea. It's a very bad idea. It's unconscionable, really, to come back into one's kitchen and find a scene like this one going on."

"Trespassers," her husband said. "Plain trespassers, that's who you are."

"Please go," Sally told them. "I'll call."

"I'm sorry," said Elizabeth.

"I'm sure you are," said Barbara. "You should have been more careful, Sally. Why invite them to *this* house?"

"Forgive us our trespasses, people. Say that three times," said Axelrod, "and see how drunk I am: trespasses trespasses trespasses. I can handle it, Ballard, can you? And what's that other word, the one you used to like to use, *transgression*, was that it?"

"Wait a minute. Hold on here."

"Transgression. You heard me. Forgive us our Press Passes. Hah!"

"Say that again," Paul Ballard said. "What did you say?"

"So what exactly, if you don't mind me asking" — Axelrod was weaving now, one hand on the counter, one sawing at air — "if you don't mind me putting it this way, just what exactly are you two doing here? Playing footsie with my girl? *Our* girl. Playing mind games by *your* rules? Why don't you run along instead, why don't you smile and just shake hands and tell everyone you're sorry and get the hell out of the kitchen? Because according to *my* script, Professor, this just isn't one of those movies where the hero comes to town and cleans up the saloon and helps some poor sheep farmer triumph over cattle barons, right, it isn't *like* that, not at all. It isn't some sweet shoot-'em-up where all the bad guys bleed ketchup and she gets to say '*My hero*,' and you ride off into the sunset and she smiles up adoringly and holds the silver bullet and there's a drumroll and then credits and slow fade. You're not the good guy, Professor, and you don't get the dame . . .

"We haven't been holding her hostage, you see. She's not here against her will. What *I* see is, the way I see it, talking about Sally, is we get to change her diapers and sit up all night worrying the day that she gets measles, we get to pay for nursery school and orthodonture and ballet class and Brearley and the prom dress and college tuition and horses and shit—not that I'm complaining, not that I mind having done it and wouldn't do it all over again—we get to be what she thinks of as *parents*, as the people who are *here* for her, the ones she can come running to and run away from when she needs to. I understand that, I do. It's part of the contract, it comes with the job.

"And I would, I mean it, I'd do it all over again, I'm ready to watch Sally go. But not to *you* two, not a pair of world-class avoidance artists like you are, because it isn't fair. I piss away my life on magazines, I write about corporate goddam America for a living and dream about junk bonds and insider trading and mergers and takeovers and suchlike, and then I come up here to find out how my daughter's doing and who she's playing footsie with, a pair of *strangers*, two goddam wannabe parents . . .

"For in case you two were wondering there hasn't been only a wedding but death in the family too. My cousin, you never knew him, Sally knew him, he lost half the side of his face. It was terrible to look at, an *af-*

fliction, there's no other word for it, is there, a cancer of the eye. It was, you know, incredibly painful but we used to go fishing together and were friends, I mean, *friends* if you know what I mean, we did everything together until the day he died. Last week. And on the day he died I was saying to Nina—that's his wife, that's who he married, when, in 1974, I remember, yes, October 22—oh, leave the man alone. Just let him go, let him quit. It's closing time; close it all down . . .

"I can see what you're thinking, I'll tell you what Barbara would say. She'd say it's all that shitty wine and all that hopefulness in Woodstock, all those J. Crew looka-likes pretending how their life is fun, pretending every time they lean so fetchingly across the split-rail fence it's for a fashion shoot. She'll tell me I'm talking too much, it's all of the shit and none of the gravy, and I'm not the right kind of host. The guy *dies*, right, he was as good as anyone and better than most with a fly rod, we used to fish the Battenkill, he doesn't only disappear and ride off in the sunset, this thing is *final*, babycakes. I mean, do you know what I mean?"

In the silence that followed he covered his eyes. Sally moved to him. "Don't worry, Dad," she said. "I promise. It's all right, I promise."

"Excuse us, please," said Barbara Axelrod. "My husband gets emotional."

"There's nothing to excuse," said Elizabeth.

"No?"

"It isn't his fault," Ballard said.

"Get out of here," said Sally.

"Why?"

"You know why."

Sam Axelrod snorted. He turned his face to the wall. Then, theatrically, he put his head in his hands and his elbows on the butcher-block table and, at the count of three, snored.

In the car, returning, the two of them were silent. He thought how many years before he first had driven her in rain and how everything had altered yet was nonetheless the same. She turned to him as if to speak, and then she turned away again and Ballard saw she had been crying and said "Please . . ."

"Please what?"

"Please don't cry."

"All right," she said. "I won't. If you say so, I certainly won't."

"How do you feel?"

"Just fine," she said. "Splendid. Terrific."

"Were you expecting something else? Somebody else, I mean."

"I wasn't expecting anything, Paul. I had no expectations."

"No?"

"Not really. Not clear ones."

"I did."

"You did?" she asked. "What sort of expectations?"

"That we'd all go to the seashore," he reminded her.

Elizabeth stared out the passenger window and he focused on the road—turning onto Route 7A, passing a chocolate barn and what used to be a gas station that now displayed antiques. "And we'd, you know, live happily . . ."

"That's *Never on Sunday*, remember. It doesn't work that way."

"No."

"Because the actress dies," she said. "She gets throat cancer or something like that. Or eye cancer, like Sam's cousin. She runs off with her hairdresser and he's a secret slasher and she ends up in a ditch."

"Don't be bitter." Ballard tried the radio but there was only static and he turned it off again.

"I'm not being bitter. A not-so-secret slasher, maybe, one who's done it often. I'm being realistic."

"Is that what you call it?"

"I do."

"Transgression," Ballard said. "It's the word they used, or I did, or *someone* did, the night that they ran over me . . ."

There was roadwork. A man in a slicker brandished a stop sign, then turned it around as they neared. A backhoe was laying down pipe.

"Sam doesn't own the word," she said. "It's only a coincidence."

"You think so?"

"Yes, that's all it is."

"She's beautiful," he said.

"Who?"

"Sally." He was out of practice in the way to pay a compliment. "She looks just the way you did. Do."

"Christ, I'd forgotten how, how *courtly* you were. Taking my arm and opening doors and bringing me flowers and suchlike. Well, don't."

"Don't what?"

"Don't start with the courtliness, please. I don't think I can bear it. Not this afternoon."

"The sun is coming out," he said. "The weather's getting better."

"That's true. Let's discuss the weather: there'll be rainbows. There's no doubt a rainbow this afternoon on the Green Mountains, Paul. If I turn my head I'm sure I can find rainbows, and the sky will be perfect, the news will be good. Why don't you just keep driving and I'll tell you what I see."

"All right."

"I see no pot of gold," she said. "No goddam Finian's Rainbow or Brigadoon or Glockamorra. Nothing cheerful, if you want to know. I think Sam told the truth."

VIII

June 14, 1996

Dear Paul:

I don't even know how to start this letter: Dear Sir,
dear Mr. Ballard, to whom it may concern? And I don't
know the right way to tell you in writing what I failed to
say at the time. When Sally slammed that door on us
(how strange it is to use those words, how peculiar to
write *us, her mother and father*), I said to myself well OK,
well why not, of course, all right, she has the right to
choose. She deserves her anger and the chance to show
it and I've no right to complain.

"Get out of here," she said. And when you asked her,
"Why?" remember, she positively hissed it: "You know
why."

But you didn't, you didn't at all.

I did.

I do.

And this isn't about our famous female solidarity or
instinctual alliance of women; I'm not trying to protect
the guilty or make some sort of claim about feminine in-
tuition as opposed to—what?—masculine bafflement.

Befuddlement. You standing there with the Axelrod clan, your face empty and expectant as a box . . .

For there's a difference, isn't there?

I knew about her all along.

Your information was one hour old.

I knew, I mean, I had a daughter.

You were, as they say, in the dark.

And what surprises me, dear Professor Ballard, is how I'd ascribed a kind of prior *knowledge* to you, a sort of habitual omniscience — as though you were my teacher still and we were in a classroom while you lectured and tamped down that pipe.

As though you surely must have known what in fact you hadn't guessed.

So the question is, why did I keep it a secret; why didn't I tell you, or write? I understood what you did not; I was conscious, you were ignorant, and that seemed so very much the reverse of how we'd behaved before that maybe I gloried in it, maybe I *wanted* a secret, a piece of privy information that you couldn't share. The rest was mostly mystery, and one I didn't try to solve until her letter came. For years I hid the knowledge or at least suppressed the fact of her existence.

Judge not lest ye be judged.

Do you know the story about the violinist who comes out to play a Bach partita, and he's no good at it but anyhow the audience applauds. This takes place in Italy where everyone's vociferous, a music critic, and they don't hesitate to make opinions known. So the performer comes on stage and takes a bow and does an encore and repeatedly butchers the music although, once more, the people in the hall applaud. He returns a third time: the entire crowd is whistling, clapping, stamping in the aisles, and so the violinist plays the piece again; it's the only one he's memorized and therefore can produce. He plays the whole thing out of tune: wrong dynamics, bowing inexact, notes missed. The lost lost lost lost chord. Nonetheless the audience pounds the floor, insisting that he come back out, and will not let him leave. But even in his grateful pride he knows he can't deserve a fifth encore, a sixth, and so he says "Ladies and gentlemen, *basta*, I've played enough Bach, I believe."

"No so," they shout. "You keep on coming out here until you get it right."

And that's what we mean by recurrence and that's why I'm writing today. I plan to stay with this until I get it right. Because I've done two things in my life from which I can't recover, for which I can't forgive myself, and you and our daughter can fix them because you're what I need.

Need?

Need.

Let's let the word stand; I need your forgiveness, and hers.

Dear Professor Ballard. Darling Paul. To Whom It May Concern. You'll have discovered, if you called the Paradise Motel, that I checked out again that night and drove off. Heading west. I just couldn't stay there, I couldn't, not after what we'd seen and heard and the way that everyone behaved. Including yours truly, of course. It's not as if, to use Sam's expression, I believed we'd ride off into the sunset and there'd be romantic music and a slow fade—not as if I *expected* a blissful reunion or thought we would go to the seashore. But it was just too rapid, too much data to absorb and news to take in all at once, and so I want to slow things down and think about what's right to do; I want to tell you where I've been and who I've been with all this time, and where Serena and Bill are at college, and what kind of house we live in and what cars we drive. I believe you do deserve that much, by way of explanation.

Oh, I've nothing to complain about, not in the world's terms, it's treated me well—far better than you did, in fact. We've been in Italy mostly. Where the people don't seem to care quite so much about rank or, let's say, the bigotry's less close to the surface and it takes a while to understand how much they despise us all—all foreigners, I mean. It's only those who qualify for their complicated gradations of "acceptable"—the ones who *might* be taken seriously—who are forced to undergo their obsessive social scrutiny and all that vicious gossip unto the sixth generation. But since we seem beneath contempt they treat us quite politely; it's their version of noblesse oblige. Be kind to little children and to foreign ladies and dogs . . .

And now I come to think of it it's more or less how *you* behaved, as if you couldn't be bothered with the difficult problem of taking me seriously, as if I might just go away because you wore kid gloves. Or if you patted me, tossed me a bone. It's a form of condescension not unlike the Italian, my love; you closed your eyes, and abracadabra o abecedarian, you could pretend it was night.

This is the sort of trip one never makes in Europe—a flat continuum, an endless open road. I arrived here late last night. And it's been exciting, a little, to find I could drive wherever I wanted whenever I wanted—while no one else knows or much cares where I am. Or when to expect me or why. Because something about what happened in Sandgate made me come across Ontario and down through Sault St. Marie—doing what I could to skirt Niagara Falls and the spectacle of honeymooners—past those Native American Casinos and the astonishing locks. I feel (how strange to feel this way again!) like my young old wandering self. I'd planned to go to Evanston, but Serena isn't leaving yet, and I do have time before she packs—a move that I promised to help her with soon. Soon enough I'll travel south.

So I'm writing this letter from Hessel, on the banks of great Lake Huron, in the Search Bay View Motel. America's full of these places, it seems, with knotty pine boards and formica countertops and cracked old leather chairs. With an office that's a breakfast nook, and an old man—equally leathery and cracked—who sits behind the counter watching TV. I'm drinking coffee yet again, from what seems like the same Styrofoam cup, with the same atrocious lukewarm silt inside it. (Italy has spoiled me in that regard, I admit; this is the sort of brew they jettison while cleaning the machines, or sluice in the gutters to drive away cats; this is the sort of place you rarely find in Umbria.) My host is watching what I think must be the local bowling channel, a lot of men in red striped shirts, taking turns as they run up the lane and stop and roll a big black ball at wooden pins. He's turned off his hearing aid, turned up the sound, and is ignoring me studiously while I pretend I'm alone . . .

A fine mist falls. The light is—there's no other word for it—green. You've not been to the Upper Peninsula, I imagine, although someday I do hope you'll come. It's beautiful here, really: the pines, the rock outcroppings, the old abandoned mines and logging trails. In my childhood I remember there were eagles that we used to watch, and deer and porcupines and moose and bear beyond counting and ducks. Take the coast of Maine and triple it and you'll have some idea of what I'm describing and what, from this window, I see.

The house. I've seen the house. Our insurance agent took me there this morning, and mostly what I felt was sheer relief. It's terrible, admittedly, but nothing like the disaster I'd imagined, and while he was bustling about, pointing out the corner where they thought soaked rags ignited, showing me the way the gong we used to ring for meals had melted—insisting how lucky we had been, how the wind that day was favorable, how there's a silver lining here and the insurance policy is full replacement value and we would be fully covered—he said, "If I were you, Mrs. Sieverdsen, if you want my advice." I didn't, of course, but he construed my silence as agreement. "I'd tear the whole thing down," he said, "and start right in again. I'd level this sucker, ma'am, it wouldn't take a dozer half a day. That way you'll have a nice *new* place, make a clean sweep."

We'll do no such thing, of course; we'll keep what's here to keep. The walls are still standing, the roof remains, the clearing kept the fire from the pine stand by the lake. We've *made* it, I heard myself saying. *Survived.*

We all seem to care about houses—Sally's parents at Sandgate, me here at the lake—as if they establish a context for or frame around the self. As if X fits *here*, Y *there*, and everything's in order and in its proper place. Yet I've begun to understand that nothing begins as we think it should start, nothing continues the way we had planned and no one knows how it will end . . .

All day, driving, I thought about children. About Sally, of course, but also her brother and sister—half-brother, half-sister—and what they would make of each other and if they'd get along. I imagined them at dinner or the beach or watching a movie or playing volleyball or something—*anything*—shared and collective; I imagined the three of them together (oh, all right, the five of us) and being *family*. It's the habit of the youthful moralist—I was one once and ought to know—to blame the evils of the world and everything that's wrong with it, the whole failed promise of creation, on those who went before. And specifically their parents. I don't know the Axelrods; as you know, we never met. Not previously, I mean. They earned the title "parents" and I relinquished my own title, "mother," the moment Sally was born. So I don't mean to try to lodge any sort of a competing claim or to defend or explain myself. It isn't my point, not at all.

Sally. Dear Sally. Our daughter. I can only imagine what the Axelrods must have gone through raising her, the pleasures of it, the rewards, and then the almost-inevitable moment she turned on them (as her half-sister and half-brother did on me, as I did earlier on my own parents) and weighed them in the balance and declared they must be wanting. Perhaps Sam drinks too much too often, and the way he behaved two days ago was simply par for the course. Perhaps Barbara has her—what shall I call it?—social rigor and sense of propriety rather too firmly in place. The Axelrods have no doubt tried but certainly failed to fix the planet and at some point I imagine Sally saying, now it's *my* turn, *my* chance.

So one fine day she looked around and said to herself, I don't belong to these people, I'm a stranger in this family, I'll find out who and where I came from and who *else* I might have been. Or maybe she complained about her parents' politics, or what they ate for dinner, or what they did and didn't do on Sunday afternoons. We all have such fantasies, don't we, we believe we're separated out at birth and (since our real parents must be revolutionaries or movie stars) need to declare our separation and say I'm after something else, I'm someone who hopes to discover her own ancestral home. In the case of adoption, perhaps, those fantasies don't fade.

Nor can they be so easily dispelled. But whatever else she might have been hoping for I'm no rich aunt from Kathmandu or great creative genius, am only the person she lately discovered—an ostrich, head buried in sand. Sally stumbled on herself, I think, by finding merely me.

We've made a mess of it, haven't we?—as did those who went before. *This* generation lives with terror so pervasive and encompassing they can't even recognize it as terror: the condition of dread. But when I first attended Catamount everyone was hopeful, everything seemed possible and everybody was convinced that things would have to change. And the agent of change could be chemical. Oh, all those monosyllables:

Weed.

Grass.

Pot.

Hash.

Coke.

Smack.

Horse.

Blow.

Dope.

The list can be lengthy—acid, psilocybin, mescaline—the point brief; we've wrecked so much that wreckage seems a habit, impossible to fix. We believed ourselves voyagers, explorers, and when you're after the expanding consciousness and standing on the threshold of a universal brotherhood, the question of who's screwing whom just doesn't seem as important or urgent as the question of who's getting screwed. We were only beginning to notice back then how "sisterhood" was mostly absent from the "universal brotherhood," how women's liberation had to deal with an old empire and overthrow it altogether in order to succeed. We went to all those meetings, looked at the men who ran them and said hey wait a minute what about the rest of us, hey, how come we get to get coffee and hustle supplies from our daddies back home and get to lie down with our universal brothers but don't make it to the microphone except maybe sometimes to sing.

But finally it did occur to us—the wide-eyed spread-legged sisterhood—that there was something wrong. The game was rigged, the scale crooked, the man in the butcher shop tilted the balance and added additional weight. So when we shook our heads at last and left the shop and started in to form our very own collectives it did seem like a revolutionary gesture or at least a political act; we didn't *need* to be bullied or brutalized, we're fifty-one percent of this nation and don't *have* to lie down and say thanks.

But you yourself were innocent. Ignorant, you'd say. Well all right you were ignorant and for so smart a man that does seem like a kind of guilt, a form of willful blindness or at least willed disinterest, and we can accuse you of that. Because things *do* change, they change. What Sally calls a power-play we called liberation; what her generation calls coercion we used to call equality, and it was a woman's right to choose. Harassment is a term of the 1990s; in the Age of Aquarius we just didn't see it that way.

I met you, remember, when I was younger than she is

today. Not twenty-one years old and a babe in the Catamount woods. I didn't regard it in that light, of course,
but believed I was ready to take on the world and ready
to win, draw, not lose. We thought we were invincible,
invulnerable, we thought—just to take one aspect of
it—that sex entailed no harm. That we'd been sold a bill
of goods by all those puritans our parents, and *Ozzie and
Harriet* and *Leave It to Beaver* and *Dennis the Menace* were
completely out of date. We thought time and the river
had altered things irrevocably and nothing would ever
be the same again and all that puritan repressiveness
was finished, over, done.

What we *risked*, I mean, seemed small. This was the
bright brief interlude, remember, when birth control
was available and syphilis wasn't a killer and no one
much knew about herpes or cared and, of course, long
before AIDS. The birds and bees were humming just
the way they did before, but the repressive fifties were
behind us and the Beats had staked a claim and then the
Beatles came along and drugs and flowers were everywhere, from Mary Jane to Lucy in the Sky with Dia-
monds, and no one had quite figured out how dangerous
they proved to be.

What did I call it, "interlude"? It's the sort of word
you liked to use; it means, I think, "between games" in
Latin, and consciousness seemed like a good thing to
change and a kind of promiscuity seemed like revolution, a way of embracing a comrade-in-arms and making
love not war. So it was pleasure, it was good clean dirty
fun, it didn't have a downside we could see.

(I can't quite believe that I'm writing to you, or writing this way about sex. And I don't intend this as some sort of confession or personal history, really, or as if I'm whispering the dirty little secrets of my own personal past. It was *impersonal*, wasn't it, a part of the general air. The two of us breathed it in along with everybody else those years, so if there's blame our daughter wants to attach—it's her right to do this, of course—then it attaches to us equally and she must blame the wind . . .)

Therefore what Sally has to understand—what I *need* her to understand—is none of this was planned. None of it, I mean, was intentional; you weren't one of those comic seducers who cackles and twirls his waxed mustachios and gets the poor girl drunk and pregnant and then gets out of town. That's so very nineteenth century, so peculiar an assumption on her part; it just wasn't the way we behaved . . .

The man at the counter gets up. He disappears behind the desk; they're running an ad for what I believe must be Designer Jeans. Children dance. A boy with no top on embraces a girl wearing only a shirt; maybe we're meant to think of them as owning both halves of an outfit. As if we can acquire two for the price of one. Next there's what I suppose to be the sound of someone showering, or using the toilet next door. It isn't the desk clerk, however; he returns with a beer in each hand and offers me a can. I smile but shake my head. He shrugs and pulls the tab off one and keeps the other also and turns up the volume: Strike, strike, spare, strike, strike.

The phone rings. He answers it, scratching his scalp. He talks about the weather, hot, the way the fish are jumping and says he can't catch shit. Then he looks at me, muttering, Yup, Ayup, and turns up the volume on the TV. I don't know why I choose to write at this round glass-topped unwiped breakfast table as opposed to the one in my room; I'm paying for that one, not this. But somehow it seems too forlorn, and even this old Yuper—that's what they call themselves in the U.P.—is better than no company at all. When the telephone was ringing I had the wild hope it would be you, Paul, calling to say, hey, I'm just around the corner or maybe come on home . . .

But of course there was the accident.

Even now, even a quarter of a century later, I can't bring myself to write about it.

Not to you.

Whose whole life would have changed, perhaps, if it hadn't happened.

If we found out who did it, and why.

Or who, by contrast, stopped to help.

If you had let me be some use to you, or if you had been in a little less pain, or even if you ever once acknowledged that I did try to assist.

Strange, the battery of studies today about battered women. Statistics on the aftermath of rape. Or what it does to self-esteem and sexuality to have been abused.

But very few studies, as far as I know, address the same problem with men.

My actual husband, Michael Vire, is a bit of a throw-back still. An unregenerate hippie of the old old school. And when and if you meet him you'll see what I'm say-ing, I think: for Michael everything's improvisational, everything renewable. He takes things as they come and go, and nothing seems to touch him much, and I sup-pose he was just what I needed—the antithesis of all that earnestness I believed came with the territory. After you and I were finished I needed a bit of a break.

The greater the cause of grief, the greater the remedy to be ap-plied. Not, however, by another but by you alone who caused it can my grief be assuaged. For it was only you who made me sad, who made me joyful or comforted me. God knows I never wanted anything more than you yourself, and I desired you purely and not for what you owned. Not for the offer of marriage, nor for anything you might provide, and not for my own passion but for yours . . .

I was working that semester on Froissart and Ville-hardouin. And I remember how you helped me with the history, pointing out the patterns and the way that roles and expectations change and then recur. Too, you made me work my senior year with the ancient Irene Gar-ber—is she still alive? I wonder—whose idea of intel-lectual instruction was a red check next to the dependent clause, a query in the margin when a colon is misplaced. Then you suggested I might also wish to study the *lais* of Marie de France and those few pre-served letters of the period in order to acquire, as it were, direct sensory experience of the literature. Re-member when you asked me if I wanted to get married I said no?

It was, I suppose, a reaction-formation, a way of saying if the thing my parents had was marriage then I wanted none of it. Or maybe I was being coy, or maybe I was just too young, or maybe it was truly how we felt those days—with our belief in liberty, free love and all the rest of it, our conviction that this sacrament would also prove passé. As if marriage was just another tradition-and-hidebound institution, another bourgeois edifice to watch come tumbling down . . .

You were a man in love with knowledge, or with a contingent reality that others call the truth. I remember how you spoke about the rush that comes with focused work, the sense of something *just* beyond our consciousness, so that *just* another stretch will do while contingent reality fades. For a moment, an instant, a heartbeat—and now I'm not discussing sex—I did feel that way. It isn't a feeling you ever forget: the sudden ideal arrangement of things, their proper alignment, the perfect if fleeting equivalence of both reach and grasp . . .

And that was what you dreamed about, what you hunted on a daily basis and more than once attained. The lover of wisdom, the *philo-sophia*, the one who *understands*. And you really were a wonderful teacher, with your grab-bag of quotations and unlit pipe waving busily, and your rigorous-seeming inquiry into the nature of truth. Your love of disputation or what we called the dialectic, your desire to argue, to point out the flaws of our logic till we learned to argue back. It was heady stuff, exciting. We saw ourselves as thinking animals and spoke about animal instinct and why *anima* might fail to rule the roost. For us, for those Catamount students who sat at your feet the gap between body and soul was a distinction we could straddle or, if we preferred to, ignore.

Once when we were making love and you had my legs over your shoulders I remember how you raised them and licked at the soles of my feet. Oh I remember everything, the feel of my toes in your mouth, the way you looked, the way you kissed them while we went on fucking though it's all those years ago. Much more than half my life. You've got your famous memory—it's photographic, nearly—and there's a lot that I've forgotten but I remember everything about the two of us. The books in your office, the books on your desk. The taste of your come, Paul, the feel of your cock in my ass. The way the meadow smelled that day, the barn you took me to the first time we went driving, the sound the crickets made, then stopped, then went on making . . .

(Oh darling, you don't want to know this. You don't need to read it; you won't; I'm writing to myself, of course, not actually writing to you. I'm sitting in the Search Bay View Motel with bowling on the TV, explaining ancient history to someone who desires or requires no explanation. Who wants to be alone.)

Yet I did choose to hide from you a central fact of your existence, an aspect of the whole that might have altered every other aspect and made you—for all practical purposes—live what you would have called untruthfully, ignorantly. In the dark. Why did I squirrel myself away—with another family and in another country—all these years? Why did I so resolutely refuse to acknowledge what we'd done? For you deserved to know, I think, that you were a father, Sally's father, and you and I had a child.

Now here's what I propose. I don't plan to return to Cortona, or not for the summer, and perhaps never again. Except to pack that place up also and shut my part of it down. It was lovely living there, it was fine for a long time but it's all over now. There's no point pretending otherwise: that part of my life is over. Finished. Done. Now what I study in Hessel is a night clerk in suspenders, drinking beer and scratching his scalp with a finger that ends at the knuckle and asking, do I bowl?

No thank you, no.

No?

No.

We had a dog in Italy, a mutt that was mostly Bouvier. With perhaps some Newfoundland thrown in. Big as houses, as you can imagine, and sweet-tempered and watchful and smelly and fierce and companionable; he lay at the foot of the stairs. He loved me unequivocally, with that no-nonsense non-provisional love that dogs accord their master. Or, in this case, mistress. Ecco took care of the children, presiding over the place, or so it seemed to me and what I gave him in exchange was food and companionship and adoration;

he lived with me eight years. And was probably two when I found him, so he died when he was ten. With his great black blotched beautiful head resting on his paws. In a kind of silence that haunts me still, won't go away, I woke up one morning and realized it had been weeks since I'd heard Ecco bark, it must have hurt him too grievously, that old loud sudden roar. That protective rumble in his throat. He died of a throat cancer, the vet said, and I felt as though it had lodged in my own throat, Paul, I couldn't swallow for sorrow, for the pure untrammeled love of him. A dog. I've never heard such a silence, not even a whimper, no sound. Those eyes staring up at me, waiting for comfort, that tail unable to wag . . .

And though they say that the best thing to do is hunt up a replacement and transfer affection I just couldn't do it, I just can't replace him. He's the dog of the universe, dog of the world. When he died so did my love of dogs, I never want another, I don't *want* to grieve a second time or ever try again. When they tell me I should try again I know there's no point in it, none.

So I've come here to ask myself what's worth the saving and what should be rebuilt. Dog, house, daughter, love. It's like that game I used to play with the two children I did raise and the jingle they chanted each summer while we watched *Sesame Street*; three of these things belong together, one of these things is not the same . . .

But in fact they *are* the same; they hang together, they're all the one form. I cannot love my house without the dog inside it; I cannot love my daughter without her father too. It all sounds so very dramatic, melo-dramatic really, but when a house is burned and it's a place the family has used for generations, for as far back as I or anyone still living can remember, there's a certain urgency. We could just let it go. Or build it back again. Which?

IX

W HEN BALLARD CALLED the next morning, Sam Axelrod answered the phone unsurprised. "It's you."

"It is. Hello."

"I figured you'd get back to me."

"That's right. And maybe you have other plans. But if you'd let me buy you lunch . . ."

"If you mean it," said the journalist. "Except I'm leaving the country on Thursday."

"For where?"

"New York. Not the country America, country Vermont . . ."

"We have to talk, we need to . . ."

"I can give you two hours, there's tennis at three. Or maybe it won't take that long."

"At noon?"

"High noon."

Ballard explained he'd be coming alone; Elizabeth had traveled on, but he was staying put. He repeated that he'd buy the lunch and was sorry to be so insistent and asked Sam where to meet.

"The Catamount Tavern. You know it?"

"Yes."

For old time's sake, said Axelrod, he'd be wearing his old Agway cap.

The Catamount Tavern was built out of stone, and there was a covered wagon in the parking lot. A display case in the entrance lobby offered souvenir tin mountain lions for sale, some in the act of leaping, others crouched as though ready to pounce. The rafters were festooned with clusters of bay leaves and myrtle wreathes and hanging pewter pots. There were banners for "Green Mountain Boys," as well as candles and maple syrup and jars of apple butter.

Ballard arrived at the restaurant first, and chose a seat facing the door. The great stone fireplace had *Warner* inscribed on its facing; it had been built by Seth Warner, a brochure at his table explained. This used to be the place he drank and courted Molly Stark. According to the local lore, Seth Warner was a great romancer as well as a great soldier, a hero of the Revolutionary War, and though there's probably no truth to the rumor that he was having an affair with Molly Stark it's nice to think they knew each other and raised a tankard or two. The tradition of hospitality first embraced by the Green Mountain Boys remains our motto here.

"Professor." Sam Axelrod offered his hand. "Sorry I'm late."

Ballard stood. The restaurant was dark, low-ceilinged, and the beams above them had been treated with what looked like creosote. Their waitress was wearing "traditional costume," a gray frock with puffed sleeves and a starched muslin cream-colored apron and cap. Her name was Jane, she informed them, and she would be their waitperson today. Ballard ordered a glass of Merlot; the journalist ordered ice tea.

Then for some minutes they spoke about the weather and the wedding Axelrod attended and how much of a surprise it was to meet again in Sandgate after all these years. He had had too much to drink, said Sam, and he wanted to apologize; his wife had informed him he'd been a disgrace. He'd taken a nap when they left, and afterwards, at dinner, Sally and Barbara both treated him like some sort of insect, a cockroach; he couldn't remember the speech he'd delivered or the way that he'd behaved. If he said anything he shouldn't have, well, blame the bad champagne . . .

"Your daughter. She's quite a young lady."

Sam Axelrod nodded.

"Our daughter," Ballard ventured. "My daughter. And why I thought we had to talk, we ought to meet for lunch like this, is that I had no idea . . ."

The waitress returned, bearing drinks. Warily he waited while she deposited their glasses and asked if they were ready to order or needed a few minutes more and smilingly assured them that they could take their time.

"Your health," said the journalist. "Ours. Bottoms up."

"We hadn't met, you understand. Well, once before, by accident. Her mother—Elizabeth, I mean—told me about her yesterday."

"You didn't know?"

"We've been"—he spread his hands—"out of touch. I didn't, no."

"Well, well," said Axelrod. "This is your life, Professor. And, yes, she's quite a girl."

"Don't call me that."

"What?"

"Professor. I haven't taught, not really, since 1970. And way back when, in Catamount, we weren't 'professors' either."

They studied their menus. They looked at the wall.

"Do you know," asked Axelrod, "that a skilled carpenter with a hand-adze can make a beam like this one"—he pointed—"look store bought-and-cut? Sawmill-square? That all this roughening, these adze marks are on the beam because they figured how the rafters would be hidden. Invisible. Or maybe they were barn carpenters, not doing finish work. So what we admire in these old ceilings is just evidenced incompetence?"

"I knew that," Ballard said.

"Of course you did, of course you do. You wrote it, didn't you?"

"I did."

"I hadn't forgotten, Professor. I was quoting from *Still Life, With Apples*. I did pay attention, you see."

The waitress flourished olive oil and poured it into saucers and described the tavern's homemade bread.

They ordered pumpkin soup. Then both of them chose the cobb salad. "An excellent choice," she declared. "It's been voted best cobb salad in the state."

At the next table a man in a pink cableknit sweater was telling his lunch partner, loudly, how the bitch had cleaned him out, how she'd taken all his credit cards and every piece of furniture and both the cars, his brand-new Beemer and the Jeep, not to mention the condo in Asheville, not to mention the CDs in their rainy-day account, but what the hey he had his health, he worked out twice a day. And no one else would look at her, would they, except for the Beemer, including that son-of-a-bitch of a lawyer she found and was paying back in Asheville on the horizontal, the bastard ought to be disbarred but, hey, the bitch was history. And what I'm telling you, he finished, is easy-come and easy-go and what the hey he had his golf clubs and was improving his game.

In the bay window parents were, or so it seemed, consoling a daughter who wept. An old, frail, white-haired woman, so bent with age she barely reached the table-top was eating mashed potatoes and what looked like fish cakes with a spoon; her companion—a young man in a bow tie and seersucker suit—kept adding butter to her plate and nodding encouragement, saying, "Granny, I promise I will." What she exhorted him to do was beyond Ballard's power to hear, but it mattered to her, clearly, for she rocked and nodded and prodded the plate repeatedly while he assured her, "Yes, Granny, I will."

Sam Axelrod finished his tea. When the waitress

came around again, he said to her, "I've changed my mind. Hell, hair of the dog. A Bloody Mary, dear." His cheeks were wrinkled, Ballard saw, as though he had lost weight or recently recovered from a sickness, and the wattles of his neck had a stiff white irregular stubble that, shaving that morning, he'd missed. Holding the glass, his hand shook. Then, smilingly, Sam leaned forward in his seat and took off his bifocals and scratched at his nose. "You had a real reason for calling, correct? Not just to plead old ignorance. If you don't mind me asking . . ."

"That time we met—not yesterday I mean but up at Harrington's, when you asked to do an interview—was it an accident?"

"Accident?"

"Yes."

"Define your terms, Professor. Do you mean coincidence?"

"No. And did you know who Sally was? Who her parents were, I mean."

"Yes."

"All the time?"

"Yes, all the time."

"Well, why did you adopt her?"

Axelrod broke a slice of bread in two and dipped it in the olive oil and chewed and wiped his lip. He drank his Bloody Mary. He licked the celery. "Penance."

"Excuse me?"

"Something like that, anyhow. Because of the trouble you found yourself in. The accident."

"The time I got hit by a car?"

"Correct."

"You knew about the car?"

Axelrod removed his cap. He twirled it; he studied it. "Yes."

"Now wait a second, let me think. Let me make sure I understand. You read about it in the paper, in the hospital admissions record maybe, or you had a friend, didn't you, Hal Robinson, who might have been aware there'd been a hit-and-run . . ."

He shook his head.

"Or were you being a, how do I put this, how did you introduce yourself, an investigative journalist?"

"No."

"A participant. A witness?"

Axelrod regarded him. "Light dawns," he said. "Now comes the dawn."

A waiter appeared with cobb salads. "Is everything all right?" he asked. "Would you care for some cracked pepper?"

"No."

The waiter withdrew.

"Tell me about it," said Ballard.

"All right."

"Where were you—were you in the car?"

Sam shook his head.

"Driving? A passenger?"

"No."

"Please *tell* me. I do need to know."

Therefore bit by bit, haltingly at first, yet with a practiced fluency that encompassed hesitation, saying, because you asked, I'll answer, Sam Axelrod did talk. This isn't easy, he declared, this is ancient history and off the record and way past the statute of limitations and just between us, understand, the two of us talking today. He and Barbara married when they both were twenty-two because she had been pregnant and then miscarried, badly, and by the time they stopped the bleeding she would never be pregnant again. You lose some you lose some, Sam said. They were living in Manhattan and her parents lived in Scarsdale and were pretty much supporting them while Barbara saw her shrink three times a week and he sat in the apartment staring at the wall. He had planned to be a writer, intending to be working on the Great American Novel, Part Two, right, *Son of Moby Dick*. He had had this idea, *long* before Benchley, that the whale could be a great white shark and there could be this loony submarine captain and Ishmael would be a cub reporter sent out to cover the story . . .

It didn't work. Mostly what Sam did instead was drink and do hackwork for magazines; he spent his mornings sleeping off the night before or singing "Hell no, we won't go," and picketing the Draft Board and pretending that he'd got 4F because they didn't want him with his capacity for troublemaking and his organizational ability, though really it was the rheumatic fever he'd been diagnosed with as a kid, left ventricle, a little leak and murmur and nothing to write home about but nothing to get drafted for either, thank heaven for small favors, the only kind he had.

Remember when I did that piece on Catamount, Sam asked, the interview when we first met, well I'd been hanging out at the college and there was this lady I found. It seems so very long ago, so far away, her name was Peg Donellen, and she had red hair. A good deal else about her was noticeable, Professor, and maybe you too noticed because Peg was hard to miss. Well, anyway, she worked in what they called the publications office, and what that mostly used to mean is that she answered the phone. She's hired as a kind of cross between receptionist and publicist, and she gets to meet this hotshot New Yorker who's doing a piece on the place. She sees me as her ticket into big-time journalism and I see her as my ticket to extracurricular ass.

I don't enjoy discussing this, I've managed pretty much to let bygones be bygones and, as they say, to let sleeping dogs lie. My marriage had been mostly grief, and what I was getting from Barbara was mostly the cold shoulder, and those were the years when everybody was into everything and it didn't seem unusual or even all that wrong. Hal Robinson had introduced us, saying we should get together for, I do think he called it, a talk. What happened to the lady of the large endowments is a mystery, Professor; she probably got married and she's probably a grandmother by now. She's maybe living in Dubuque and a fundamentalist or maybe she did hook the next available hotshot and lives in California with a houseboy and a face-lift; I don't know, I really don't care. It's water way under the bridge.

So I'm working on this story about town-gown relations, about a place where one single tuition equals the annual salary of those local folks who work there, mowing lawns or in the kitchens or the power plant. I'm up here, staying in Sandgate—it's been in Barbara's family forever, they call it their old summer place—and doing this story on Catamount and driving down for interviews; you don't need any details but we'd parked there the night of the crash. Because after work maybe three weeks earlier the ambitious and lonely and enthusiastic Ms. Donellen has inquired if I'd care to look a little more closely into the question of town and gown relations, with particular reference to what's underneath the gown. I'm not being fair, I suppose. I suggested she invite me, and two or three times that spring we held what Peggy liked to call our in-depth interviews . . .

So there was this place in the woods. There was this tree she liked, she liked it up against a tree, and afterwards we're walking down and I'm already late and in a rush. I can't help it, when I talk to you I get this way: it's Aristotle, isn't it, what did he say, Professor? *Post coitum omne animalia* desires to go home to bed and learn how to cover his tracks . . .

The waitress returned. "Is everything all right?" she asked.

"Just fine," said Axelrod. "Fine."

"Can I get you anything? Another Bloody Mary, sir?"

"You can get the hell out of here, darlin'," said Sam. "You can let us eat our meal."

And then he told the story of the Good Samaritan, saying he had been that man—you get it, Sam Samaritan, your humble servant, sir. First "a certain man" is set upon by robbers and beaten and left in a ditch. Maybe they think he's dead, maybe they leave him there to die, maybe it doesn't matter once they steal his cash and mule. Then other travelers use the same road and see him lying by the side of it but fail to heed his cry for help or, if they hear it, pass carelessly on. They refuse to get *involved*. But finally a Good Samaritan takes pity on the man and gets down off his trusty steed and helps the injured fellow ride and brings him into town.

Jesus tells this story as a parable of decency, of how to get to heaven when you're traveling alone. I've never drowned, in point of fact, I've never been a drowning man, but what they report is how the life you've lived gets played out all over again. If you drown, of course, it's over, but if you float or get rescued or whatever then you have a second chance; you get a new beginning and get to start over again.

And that's what it felt like out there in the road, the journalist said, leaning back in his chair, as though everything I'd been and everything I'd done was finished, and all of it would recommence and be altogether different from the way it was before. Now he, Sam, liked to think the two of them, that evening in the GTO, could qualify as Good Samaritans, though they'd also been the Philistines up there behind the barn. It's what they call a pivot point, a revelation, if you don't mind me mixing up or what we call in the business cross-referencing my sources. My mixing them, I know what you're thinking, *my mixing*, a gerund, correct. Which is also why I was a little bit, well, taken *aback* when you walked into the house or when I walked into it yesterday and you were sitting there . . .

In point of fact it took Sam longer than it should have, probably, to get the point, to get with what Barbara called the program and understand how it was something to go home for, something to try for called decency, focus, and something to work at together until they worked it out. He never saw Peggy again. He never wanted to. When they dropped Ballard at the hospital it was over, it was finished, it was like Sam saw a sign. There but for the grace of God, et cetera, it might have been me who was bloody and wrecked; it might have been you driving by. And every single day of his life from that night of his life he himself had been, if not stone sober, straight; he'd walked the straight and narrow ever since. Because I had, hey, a conversion, a religious experience right then and there by the side of the road; I picked you up sidesaddle and put you on my mule. I just slung you in the backseat, pal, and carried you to town.

The very old lady behind them wheeled back from her table tremblingly. Her grandson stood behind her chair and guided her into the lobby, then out of sight.

"Are you finished, gentlemen?" the waitress asked.

Ballard shook his head.

"More water, sir?" she asked.

Sam Axelrod waved her away. My dad was Jewish and my mother's Catholic, you see, or both of them were raised that way until they both turned atheist and married in the thirties, when it was still okay to be a Communist or at least a socialist, when religion was the people's opiate, according to Karl Marx. And it still is, far as I'm concerned, but don't go telling that to Billy

Graham or Pat Robertson and Jerry Falwell and their gang; it gets you thrown out of the party. The Republican Party, I mean. But all it got *me*, when they got over being socialists, having heard about the gulag and the dicey way that Stalin dealt with opposition, what I got by way of inheritance was a dose of guilt. Guilt from the Catholic, shame from the Jewish half: put them all together they spell penance, redemption, the not-so-wholly abstract entity we've just been discussing, the works . . .

So I thought to myself, I can remember thinking, shit, he knows Hal Robinson, he maybe won't get better and I better go find out. And then I called the hospital but for obvious reasons I couldn't visit because we hadn't been as you might say formally connected in the woods that night. Except it was an open secret that you had that girl, and everybody in the college knew, and Peggy knew, and the final time we talked, when I called her the next afternoon to say goodbye and call it quits she gave me Elizabeth's name. So it wasn't very difficult to find out what was going down and where she went and what she took along with her when she got out of Catamount. I was married and in trouble, and Barbara's shrink had said that we should try again, there was nothing like a kid to fix what ailed her, depression without a postpartum was how the shrink expressed it, I think, but then her other doctors said don't bother there's no point.

Well if your folks are Barbara's folks and you want to fix your daughter it isn't that hard to arrange. They knew people in Grosse Pointe Farms and the people in Grosse Pointe Farms knew people in Grosse Pointe

Shores, and from then on it's a matter of like attracting like, of taking care of business with your business partners, really, since we wanted what the Sieverdsens most definitely did *not* want, and couldn't use, and there were intermediaries and the simple problem of an airplane to Detroit, two people flying west and then three of us coming back east.

Professor, if you don't know what it feels like you can't imagine something that young on your shoulder, something so sweet in your arms. Add the diaper and receiving blankets and the outfit that they'd put her in and the bundle was maybe ten pounds. Sally. Our Sally. My kid. I remember, what's the word, *bonding* with her on the plane, whispering to her the whole way back, it's all right, okay, you'll be fine now, you're welcome, you're safe. And then there were those years with her growing, all those cups she'd bang on the tabletop, words she would learn to pronounce. The teddy bears, the ballet school, the whole entire works. How proud we were the day she figured out what part of her mouth was the place to put food in, and smile, and how to hold a spoon, the day she produced her first sentence—*Mommy want a cracker*, or maybe *Polly wants a Mommy*, that was it . . .

So when my daughter asked me to find out about her folks, her birth parents, I knew who they had been, of course, I didn't have to do the looking I pretended for her sake. But I couldn't bring myself to name your name, to include you in, since as far as I could tell your girlfriend never gave you what I guess we'll call the chance. We all just included you out. And so what really happened was—there's no other word for it—a saving grace, a symmetry, since when you put your burden down I lifted it instead. You saved me the way I saved you. Because otherwise I'd be forgotten bones and wasted opportunity and buried shit by now. But what I am is grateful, what you've given me is Sally and the chance to be a father and play Sam Samaritan. So I'm your worst nightmare, Professor, I'm your post-traumatic recall come to ask forgiveness, and let's split the cost of this lunch. Or let me invite you, okay?

The journalist excused himself; he went to the bathroom and said, I may play tennis, after all, I could use the exercise. Their waitress brought the bill and, by the time Paul Ballard walked to the cash register and paid and, blinking in the sudden light, watching a tour bus pull into the driveway, emerged into the air again, Sam Axelrod was gone.

That night he called the house in Sandgate; Sally answered. He spoke about his lunch, and how he and Sam had talked, and she said, yes, she knew. When Ballard said they too had things to talk about and asked to see her she agreed, although not until her parents left for Manhattan on Thursday. Where would you like to meet, he asked, and she said this time I'll come to *your* house. You've been here once before, he said, and she said, yes, I remember the porch but not how to get there, of course. It was too long ago, he said, and then he gave her directions and she said, how about Thursday for tea.

"Tea?" Ballard repeated, and she said, "Fine, at four o'clock. I'll be there. I can drive."

At four o'clock precisely the Range Rover pulled up. He watched her descend from it, long-legged, lithe, and shaking her hair loose as though for a photographer; she carried a black leather backpack and was wearing blue jeans, a tank top, and clogs. Like the image of Elizabeth she approached the place he waited, and her stride was her mother's own stride.

"You made it," he said. "Was it easy to find?"

"Yes."

"Well, welcome. Do come in."

She angled past him in the hall and, while he held the door for her, entered Ballard's library. When she shrugged herself free from the backpack it was as though the motion had been studied for effect. "Is this the place you write your books?"

Speechless, he nodded.

"That table, there?"

"Yes."

"I wondered," Sally said.

There was nothing he knew how to say. That morning he had purchased tea, Earl Gray and Lapsong Souchong, together with the various decaffeinated teas that Mrs. Harrington informed him people were drinking these days: Yellow Zinger, Blackberry, Lemon, Rose Hip, Chamomile. He arrayed these tea bags on a tray, together with sugar and two kinds of milk. He had bought cookies also, and muffins and macaroons and a chocolate cake and cheeses and peanuts and cashews and jam; he had the kettle boiling by three-thirty, and he set two places at the dining-room table, from which he cleared files and books.

Dust danced in the light of the windows, and he wiped the table repeatedly and swept and mopped the room; he stopped himself from washing the windows only with an effort, and only after running out of Windex on the second pane. He did not have time to weed the flowerbeds or mow the lawn, and he reproached himself for what he now saw, bitterly, as seediness and long neglect; the house required painting and the roof should be reshingled and the gutters cleaned.

Sally noticed none of this or, if she noticed, did not complain. Some part of Ballard understood that she had decided to charm him and was playing the ingenue's role. She examined the bookshelves respectfully and pored over his few photographs, and praised the Kelim rug. Of the Grandma Moses in the dining room—a charcoal drawing of a rooster he had bought in 1968— she inquired, "Is that real?" They spoke about the time she'd arrived at his house a dozen years before, and what a strange coincidence it now appeared to be. "Do you think it *was* coincidence?" she asked.

"How do you mean?"

"I don't mean, oh, I planned it. Or that anybody did. I mean, do you think there was some larger, some . . ."

"Purpose? A shaping intention?"

"Right. A *plan*."

"Do you?"

Sally chose a macaroon. Her fingernails, he saw, were

bitten to the quick. "I don't like to think that way. I'm not, I mean, superstitious."

"It's the great blessing and curse of modernity," Ballard ventured, "coincidence. It's the Uncertainty Principle as first defined by Heisenberg. And it's the difference, if you will, between event and plot: when there's not so much a hidden meaning or a code to crack as meaning that we tease out afterwards in order to *order* experience." He poured. "To confer some kind of clarity in retrospect, to counteract uncertainty—for it isn't always obvious to those of us engaged in action what the act itself is likely to result in. So we offer up an explanation that's both necessary and sufficient—most people used to call it God—a pattern to the story that might otherwise seem random."

"You really were a teacher," Sally said.

"Yes. I'm sorry, I don't mean to lecture. When I'm nervous I clam up or talk . . ."

"What do you mean, 'uncertainty'?"

Encouraged, he continued. "Well, what Heisenberg discovered is that the act of observation alters the thing seen. As soon as you examine what's in the *process* of happening you become a part of the equation, and its components will change. 'The unexamined life is not worth living,' says Socrates—or, more properly, Plato said Socrates said it—but life changes while you watch. 'A watched pot never boils,' remember, contains its own contradiction and it makes sense both ways. In one version it can mean please keep the pot from boiling because it's wise to remain watchful, or in another version the moral of the saying is 'leave well enough alone.' "

"When I remember that visit," she said, "it's like, what's the expression, oh, déjà vu all over again."

In companionable silence, then, they drank their tea. "I don't think it was planned," he said. "But I'm very glad it happened. And that you're here today."

"Well anyway," she said. "I'm grateful to my parents. They *are* my parents, understand, it's just I'm glad to meet you too."

"I understand," he said.

He was embarrassed by his outburst, Heisenberg and Plato trotted out for her inspection while he tried to prove a point. Her behavior was attentive and her attitude expectant, as though she were ready to answer what he could not bring himself to ask: *Do I disappoint you; what is it, Daughter, you want?* He had been planning to explain and, in conscious replication of the speech he'd heard from Axelrod, unburden himself to the girl. Instead he poured a second cup and said, "There's marmalade" and brushed at his mouth with his hand. He shared more blood with Sally—this nearly total stranger—than any living person in the world. Yet he knew little of her history and she did not know him at all.

"It's hard," she said, "to figure out. I mean, to know what we should talk about . . ."

Therefore haltingly he spoke once more: I owe you what I want to call my story, though it has little action or plot. Like you and like your mother, I was an only child. And when we met I was, oh, how to put it, self-absorbed to a degree that still amazes me; I didn't *imagine*, you understand, I never even guessed you were conceived. Conception—Ballard smiled at her—the great word of art and of life. Well, I hadn't the foggiest, had no conception, I was this very clever and well-educated ostrich, head buried deep in the sand.

Your mother plays a part in this, of course. She tried to stay with me during what we called my convalescence, my recuperation, and if she'd stayed a little longer or I'd looked a little harder I might perhaps have noticed. But she didn't tell me and I didn't ask and we were, as the saying goes, two ships that passed at night. Because I felt—oh, Sally, it's hard to explain what I felt—*estranged* from my own existence, not to mention hers, or yours, or any other creature's; I became a kind of monk. I missed my chance, *our* chance, and it's not the sort of thing you get to do over again.

"The Uncertainty Principle," Sally said. "When you look you change things . . ."

"Yes."

"I'd nearly given up," she said. "I didn't think it would be useful."

"What?"

"To find out who you were. To look for you. Or for my mother either."

"I'm very glad you did," he said. "More tea?"

She shook her head. "I'd better leave."

"So soon?"

"Before you tell me to. Because I've gotten touchy," Sally said, "about desertion."

Paul Ballard shut his eyes. Attempting to clear it, he pressed both hands to his head. In the last days his entire world had shifted on its axis, and all his assumptions proved wrong. He'd met Elizabeth and learned they had a child; he'd met the child and learned that her adoptive father had been in the woods that night and, atoning for old infidelities, had raised the girl. He who thought himself acute as witness had discovered the reverse; he had been self-deluded and, when it came to self-scrutiny, blind . . .

What can I say, he asked himself, what explanation offer that will not sound self-serving? On this shelf are seven inches of my life's work: words. It's a peculiar thing to labor at and try to make important; it's so small a thing to accumulate and say "This is the sum and substance of my knowledge: what I knew."

So he told her of his years alone and his hopes and expectations and the way they'd been fulfilled or failed, his dream of reputation and how it faded over time: his fierce embrace of privacy that had become mere pride. He felt, again, displacement—that old familiar sense of being advocate and audience, at one and the same time both lawyer and judge. "I'm not such a monster, am I?" asked Ballard, and she said, smilingly, "No."

"I'm only," he told her, "a fool."

X

ELIZABETH DROVE BACK. This time she took the southern route—dropping down through Michigan and Ohio until the New York Thruway where she started seeing double outside of Buffalo and spent the night in Batavia. The girl behind the motel counter had been talking on the telephone, and she produced the registration card and room key while cradling the receiver, talking, nodding, saying at intervals, "Can you believe it? Be*lieve* it? Oh my God."

Elizabeth paid up in cash. In the room she fell asleep at once, dreaming travel-haunted, fitful dreams, and woke to the sound of her neighbor's TV, and then to a shower, then shouting, and then again what sounded like TV. There was music and canned laughter and applause. She had not expected to sleep well or long, but she had been more tired than she knew and when she woke the sun was bright and, already at ten o'clock, high. There were fire engines in the motel parking lot, and several police cars also. It took a minute to determine that there had been neither a fire nor an accident but that the firemen and policemen outside her window were selling tickets to some sort of raffle or county fair or dance, and that the members of the 4-H Club would wash her car for free. She drank coffee from the apparatus in the bathroom—a two-cup Mr. Coffee with a filter packet and a plastic spoon for stirring and containers of nondairy product powder and an assortment of sweeteners—and packed and returned the room key and, walking to her car, found children preparing to wash it. She told them, "Don't bother, it's rented," but they laughed happily and said, "We want to, we're *supposed* to, Mrs., it's fun." Holding her bags, Elizabeth waited while they soaped and scrubbed and hosed her car, and then she gave them five dollars, which was the suggested donation, and waved at the nearby policeman and continued east.

The road was flat and straight; she passed a turf farm and a quarry and a wildlife sanctuary, and by one o'clock she stopped for gas near something called the Electronics Highway, outside of Syracuse. There, standing at the self-serve pump, preparing herself for what would come (watching a fat man in a T-Shirt that read *Under This, I'm Naked*, listening to his car's radio and the insistent beat of what she came to recognize as shouted rhyme, two singers repeating in unison, "Hey baby baby baby maybe you and me can make a baby," hearing the full-throated whine of the trucks, the pickups and the buses and the station wagons screaming past), Elizabeth asked herself where she was going, and what was the necessity of going back to Catamount, and why.

Light-headed she paid the attendant. Then she idled for some minutes at a grassy strip beyond the pumps, near a trash can and a picnic bench and two women walking their dogs. The women appeared to be strangers, but their dogs were eager, sniffing, straining at their leashes. "Is that a golden?" the older woman asked. "No, Jessie's a field lab," the younger one said. "But she gets this bladder infection and we need to stop every ten minutes, it seems like, and my husband's fixing to shoot her. It's what he tells me, every time. Or maybe he'll just drive away . . ."

America, America: Beth tried to calm her breathing and control her rising fear. She rested her head in her hands. Now by an act of concentration—or, rather, by an act of focused willed forgetfulness—an image of Cortona came to her where she sat. It would be early morning at the farm, and she and her dog shared the kitchen; upstairs, the children slept. In her vision she was young again and Ecco in his massive prime, and she was standing by the AGA, making jam. The shelf where she arranged the jars grew redolent with figs, and she could *smell* them, nearly, and their skins felt cool and slippery and the basin where she pulped the seeds was sticky-sweet and glistening, and everything she touched was hers and all of it familiar . . .

"Get *in* here," someone shouted. "Get that fucking dog in the *car!*"

America, America: she tried to shut it out. There was music on the radio: the duet from *Otello* at the finale of Act One. The violins trembled, soared, sank. *Un baccio*, the tenor demanded, and after Desdemona offered it up yieldingly he asked for and received a second kiss. Light slanted through the window—not the thruway's mechanical glare but the soft gleam of Tuscany—and the concrete abutment by her side seemed as paving stones wet with dawn dew . . .

"Get *in* here, I'm warning you. Shut the damn *door*!"

She slathered fig jam on dark bread and offered a biscuit to Ecco who was lying at her feet. He pricked up his ears, thumped his tail. He looked at her adoringly and took the biscuit from her hand with jaws that could snap it in two. He was hoping for his morning walk and full of expectation; he would lie at her feet till she took off her apron and shook out her hair and said, "Come!" Why not return to what she knew, Elizabeth wondered, and live surrounded once again by olive groves and meadows and the trappings of her comfort in that lovely private place; why not shop for meat and chocolate at the bottom of her hill? Why could she not go home?

The answer arrived with the asking; it had never been her home. Her beloved ancient Ecco, her faithful companion, was dead. The man called Michael Vire to whom she had been married was a nearly total stranger, and together they produced two children who were also strangers now. Serena and Bill had departed, as was right and proper, and it would be futile to return. If she herself went back to Italy the people of the village would be surprised and voluble, would tell her what was happening and what had failed to happen to that history teacher who slandered the Pope, and in great and extravagant detail would describe the fire in the garage of the Carabinieri last August that they had information had been paid for by the mayor's wife, *certo, e vero*, they would shake their heads and say she must be tired from the journey, *evidammente*, and should have a coffee with perhaps a little grappa. Had Elizabeth heard and did she know that Lydia the cleaning woman contracted *il focco di San Antonio*? a torment, Saint Anthony's fire, what the English call the shingles, and was absolutely immobile and lay in her dark room all day with a cold compress on her face, on top of the sheets, *la poverina*, and could not clean the house. But it could be arranged, of course, Lydia's sister was available and would be happy to work as a substitute until her sister got over the illness, the suffering, *dio, dio*, how she suffers, so that in time to come as time before the business of business as usual would be simple to resume; the garage could be remodeled, or the pump house by the pool. She could work something out with Michael, a living arrangement not so very different from the ménage they had managed all these years; he and his lover and the children (home for vacations, for holidays, briefly) would get along just fine . . .

The terror subsided; she opened her eyes. There was nothing to return to but her actual destination: North Catamount, Paul Ballard's arms. Elizabeth continued; she started the car and drove on.

Arrived, she checked in once again at the Paradise Motel. She called him and he came. This time there was no argument nor any hesitation; he embraced her, and she him.

"Well, here I am," she said, and he said, "Yes, you are."

Awaiting his arrival, she had dropped and closed the blinds. She had used the toilet and turned off the bathroom light. "I won't ever let you go," he said, and she said, "Not again."

They kissed. His breath was stale. "This is so strange," he said, "I'm nervous, are you nervous?" and she answered, "Yes."

As though by unspoken agreement, they moved towards the bed. He was clumsy, a little, untying his shoes, and she found herself remembering how many years ago she first had noticed that—the way he exhaled, bending over, the way he reversed his socks, pulling them down.

"I don't know what to do," he said. "I don't know what we ought to do."

Removing her half-slip, she stood. Now briefly she too lost her poise and did not want him watching her, the contusion at her ankle and where her waist had thickened, the stretch marks William gave her in her final pregnancy and how her thighs had spread. She placed her fingers on his eyes and, lightly, softly, pressed.

"You're beautiful," he said, and Elizabeth laughed. "I'm the one who adores you," he said.

In the next minutes, repeatedly, she wondered what would happen if they stopped. While turning down the sheets she knew that she could still refuse, might pull away and tell Ballard to leave her or, failing that, leave by herself . . .

"Are you all right?" he asked.

"I'm fine," she said. "Are you?"

"There isn't any choice," he said, and she said, "No, no choice."

Ballard made a sound deep in his throat. Yet if she could she would have willed a total silence on them, a room beyond the reach of gravity where they could hide together until the crack of doom. He stiffened against her; she reached for his shoulder and stroked the small bones of his back. She heard herself crying; she kissed his cold neck.

"I've missed you," he whispered. "I missed you so much."

"Don't say that," said Elizabeth, "you don't know what you're saying," and he put his old man's mouth upon her fallen breast. As though from a great height, she studied where they lay. Now what she felt was mostly grief, the rank whiff of their bodies and the unfamiliar way he moved and the decades passed. In darkness, on her shabby bed, they rehearsed the shared language of sex. For his sake, she pretended; she rocked and gasped and slipped his penis into her with the appearance of pleasure. The love they made was tentative, uncertain in its rhythm, and it was over quickly and she could not come.

She needed a shower; she wanted to sleep. He pulled away and heaved down by her side and stared at the ceiling and asked "Are you all right?"

She said "Yes."

"Do you mean it?" he asked, and she put her finger on his lips.

To Ballard their meeting was shock after shock: a quarter of a century since he had held her, anyone, or brought himself to climax in this fashion. He lay with his forearm thrown over his eyes and, shivering, tried to establish some sort of composure. His heart was pounding and his jaw hurt from how he had clenched his teeth, coming, and his tongue tasted of blood. His wrist hurt and his knees ached from the way he had balanced above her, and semen still leaked from his cock. "I love you," he said.

"It's okay," said Elizabeth. "You don't have to say that."

"I do."

"It's okay," she said again. "We're just out of practice, Paul."

He tried to laugh and could not. "I've loved you all this time," he said. "I never loved anyone else."

"You're being sweet."

"It's true. I didn't always know it, but it was always true."

"Who was it—was it La Rochefoucauld?—who said far fewer women would allow themselves to be seduced if they received compliments standing. If people praised them just as much while they were dressed and vertical. So we lie down for flattery . . ."

"I can't remember."

"Michel de Montaigne?"

"You're beautiful standing," he said.

"I thought about us often. I thought what we would do and say and what it would be like and feel like." She propped herself up on her elbow. She studied him. "I thought about it all the time, and now I don't know what to want, I don't know what you want with me . . ."

" 'A woman,' said Montaigne," he said, " 'ought to remove her modesty when she takes off her clothes.' "

She laughed. He could feel his spirit lighten and his anxiety ease. He kissed her cheek, her neck. "Are you all right?" he asked. Elizabeth caressed and rose above him archingly and folded herself down again and ran her tongue along his prick so as before he was aroused and entered her, although with less blind urgent need, with more attention to her own, his eyes accustomed to the dark, his body beginning to move with assurance and lead where she followed and follow her lead, their old salt rhythm in the sheets—"Oh Paul," she sang to the pillow, "Paul, Paul!"—and he raised her legs across his shoulders in the way he used to, driving, plunging, crying out, and lost the sense of where he was, and when, and lost the sense of loss, time passing and their bodies' force, and gloried in the sight of her, the taste and touch and smell and sound, and everything was in his reach and in his grasp and all of it was, finally, redeemed.

In the morning, while he helped her pack, when they touched or brushed past each other in the narrow space between the motel bed and window, such contact felt familiar. Or, as they assured each other, things could return to a *status quo ante*, square one. She had asked him not to spend the night, to let her have some breathing space in what she now called, only half-jokingly, Paradise; she needed sleep, she said, and with you here my darling, it would be difficult, impossible; I need to pinch myself and make certain it isn't a dream. It isn't a dream, Ballard said, it's the actual astonishing truth.

At lunchtime they drove to his house. There were drawers to empty and roofs to repair and the vegetable garden to tend to and the apple orchard to prune. There was a cobweb or twenty to dust, a fresh coat of paint to apply. He had been impersonating Winckelmann, he joked, old Rip Van Ballard asleep at the wheel, and had been on automatic pilot for too long. If she had no objection to a scholar's temporarily shabby abode, would she consent to share it with him and, as he suggested once before, become his wife?

No objection, delighted, said Beth. They made love again, upstairs. A beam of dust-illumined light lay slantways on the bed, and he told her he had been a celibate, entirely, since she left. I was saving myself, Ballard said, and his attempt at humor made her smile. She was happy, she told him, happy, happy, and in the due and proper course of things would return her rented Hertz and institute divorce proceedings and introduce him to the children, to William and Serena; they would all get along, she was sure. Were any of their old friends here, did he have friends, did he have enemies? Did he still own an apple press and should they give a cider party in the fall? She would scrub and clean and air out the shelves in the pantry, and wasn't that her old coat hanging in the closet, the one with the red patches so that no one might mistake her for a deer? She had arrived in Catamount with only one suitcase and a garment bag, but at the end of the week she arranged for shoes and clothes and cosmetics to be shipped to America from Italy, as well as those belongings she could not bring herself to live without—the children's photograph albums, the pillow Serena embroidered with a heart and inside it an arrow and reading *Love you, Mom.*

They planned to fly to Milano together and drive south and collect the rest of her belongings from Cortona. They would do so in the fall—October, November perhaps. But Elizabeth had passed the stage, she told him, where material things seemed important, or when she needed to accumulate objects in order to believe that she herself might be objectively of value. It was how she'd felt in the last years of her marriage, and all the more so, paradoxically, since Michael liked to say that money was irrelevant and he'd have proposed to her twice as quickly if she were half as rich. He declared this with a negligence, a studied inattention that signaled its own opposite: he was one of those men to whom money meant little or nothing as long as he never needed it, and he hadn't needed money because she wrote the checks. Responsibility, she said, was never Michael's strong suit, but it's over now, all over now, it doesn't even seem to me it ever mattered much . . .

For the first days and weeks, with a passionate retentiveness, Elizabeth tracked their shared steps. I need, she said, to locate every single footprint in my personal memory lane, I want to haunt our old haunts. He would not take her to visit the college, and she said she understood but drove there by herself and walked through the classrooms and the library and Commons building and, pretending to be a present student's mother, her old dorm. She made him take her to the barn where they had first become lovers, and when he said it burned down years ago, I read about it in the paper, she said let's find it, anyhow, let's please go look. If you insist, said Ballard, and she said I do insist. They wandered the back roads of Catamount—not dirt any longer but wide and well paved–where on that fateful afternoon they drove together, in the rain, and found the structure had indeed been destroyed, and what remained of it were only dismantled foundation stones and a latticework of vines. It doesn't bother me, she said, it makes no difference, really, but the thing that's astonishing is one night in Cortona I was certain it was burning, it felt as though there were a conflagration in my head, I believed at the time it was Hessel but it must have been this barn. Or maybe both of them at once, oh isn't it astonishing to be back here again.

He had attended D. A. Fulbert's funeral that week. In the years of their association he had known the man only as "Dean," but the *Catamount Clarion* described the deceased as "Daniel Astrolabe Fulbert, known to his many friends as Danny." According to the newspaper, Dean Fulbert was seventy-nine. He was survived by his fourth wife and a son, Daniel Jr., of Spokane. The obituary notice listed the deceased's accomplishments and where the service would be held and asked, in lieu of flowers, that contributions should be made to the Holbein Memorial Hospital Outreach and Hospice Program.

The auditorium was full. Those who came to honor Fulbert spoke of him at length. At intervals a woman in a green dress stood up and sang the folk songs of her native Silesia; after her first mourning song, an electrified wheelchair advanced. It settled next to Ballard, in the aisle. He recognized its occupant as Jason Newcomb, the final incapacitated survivor of the family he had described in *Still Life, With Apples*.

Newcomb rocked. Spittle gathered in the corners of his mouth. He sat in the wheelchair, humming to himself; his hands grappled with the armrests continually. He wiped his mouth with his tie and, leaning forward, farted; the smell was intense. The woman sang of cradles rocking in the dark wood where my lover lies, his heart like the heart of the oak. She lifted her imposing arms on the high notes. Her hair was black. She sang about the shape of death that comes to us so suddenly, and used to be a bird and now impersonates a dog.

Jason Newcomb rolled his head. Something had exploded near him in Phnom Penh—a mine or possibly a shell fragment or strafing fire from a plane or helicopter.

His eyes were closed; he beat time with his right hand, ponderously. There were two fingers missing. The woman sang of life's long rest, and she finished with a cry that lingered in the air. Then she was supplanted by representatives of Catamount College. They spoke of the dean's impassioned advocacy of the faculty, his skills in labor arbitration and strong sense of duty. Even on his dying day, D. A. Fulbert rose at dawn to read the morning paper. He went to lunch as he had always gone to lunch, at 11:45; he ate what he usually ate. He was gracious to the waitress, he was gracious on the phone. They were convinced, they said, he met his last appointment with his customary grace.

Paul Ballard rose to leave. He excused himself as quietly as possible. Standing, however, he jostled the chair; heads turned. And for an instant, abruptly, he could not remember the dean's name, nor the function of the committee on which they once had jointly served, nor why he had come to the service. He had had some purpose. Someone had suggested he attend. He had chosen to, had had his reasons, had appointments to cancel or keep. He walked through the lobby, starting to panic, shoes squealing as though they were wheels.

In September Elizabeth planned a surprise. I don't like surprises, he said, I've had enough surprises in my time, and she said "Trust me, Paul." On the occasion of his birthday she drove him to Equinox Mountain, where they first ate together in public in 1969. Although a sign proclaimed *New Management*, the waterfall was still in place; they sat at a table by the window where the two of them had celebrated her coming of age, and the food was much the same. Elizabeth ordered a Pouilly Fumé; it's what we drank that night, she said, remember? How do you know what we drank, he asked, and she said I remember it all. I remember every single thing we ate and drank and everything you said.

This was, he came to understand, the truth. Verbatim, she repeated what he'd once declared in class or on Commons Lawn or driving from the hospital or on the telephone. And he, whose memory had served him well, whose recall was nearly total, felt ashamed or at least inattentive by contrast; what was vivid to Elizabeth remained, for Ballard, blank. His accident had functioned as a fulcrum and a pivot point, a kind of *before* and *after*, and he had schooled himself in inattention. In a chapter of *The Mind and Its Inscape* he had even argued for oblivion's utility and the healing usage of forgetfulness.

Little by little, however, as she settled in again, as his routine of work resumed, the past grew available to Ballard too. He played his guitar for her, and she listened with her eyes half-closed, tapping her fingers, nodding, smiling. "Do you remember?" she would ask, and he would answer "Yes."

The figure a chiasmus makes, a phrase turning back on itself.

A square of Hershey's chocolate melted in his fist.

His delight in Scriabin at ten.

His grandfather's chair where the old man sat smoking.

A Montecristo. Schimmelpenninck. White Owl.

His science teacher showing how the earth moves round the sun. A waste basket, a flashlight, the blackboard, some string.

The way his mother would rub cold cream into her palms nightly and, taking off her rings, anoint her fingers after doing the dishes, then her cheeks, the glistening dank sweetness of it when she bent down above him for his night-night kiss.

Wenn Man eine Operation durchgemacht hat, dann braucht Man Erholung. After a person has had an operation, the person requires time to recover.

The quadratic equation. An infinity sign. The certainties of algebra, the sense that things make sense.

Except perhaps for i, the imaginary number which, when multiplying its own negation, minus one times minus one, remains nonetheless a negative.

The slap of fist on leather, bat on ball.

The way a line drive rises, falls, the way a grounder, bouncing, bounced.

The sacrifice of queen's rook for a bishop, and then the queened pawn.

Ginger ale and ice cream, vanilla of course. Or root beer and chocolate, or soda water and coffee, it's what we call an egg cream, not an ice-cream float.

Excuse me, Mr. Miller, if everything Before Christ happened prior to the Year One and if everything After Death happened after the Year One, then how could He have lived?

The elongated face and hands of an El Greco peni-
tent.

His teacher's dismissive response. It doesn't mean
that, Paul, it means Anno Domini. In the year of our
Lord. A.D.

The Rondonini Pieta. The pottery at Vallauris.

But B.C. means "Before Christ," right? And it's *English*, Mr. Miller, why would they shift out of English to
Latin like that?

The light in Caravaggio, Correggio, Memling, the
source of it. Lucas Cranach the Elder. Andrea Man-
tegna. Hieronymus Bosch.

The stones of the combe that he hiked through on the
way to Stonehenge in, when was it? 1956.

The Tiepolo ceilings at Würzburg. The Peter Paul
Rubens at Whitehall.

The Ruy Lopéz opening, the Capablanca defense.

The second movement of Mahler's Fifth Symphony,
the Schubert Impromptus, the two Mozart piano quar-
tets.

His first champagne. White wine in her glass in the
kitchen that night. The cheese labelled *Caprice de Dieu*.

Aristotle Contemplating the Bust of Homer. Discovered, queried, ratified, agreed-upon, sold, bought.

His father's daily newspaper, the way that he folded it
over into quarters and, after reading, smoothed each
crease.

His early engagement, his wife, her hay fever, her
love of dry toast.

Their almost total (except once, at sunset, her arm at
his waist) incompatibility.

Did she call it, or did he imagine this, *actualize*? Self-actualize?

And did the man she married afterwards get elected to the State Assembly or the Senate; did he build that shopping mall; do they live happily?

The apple tree, the singing, and the gold.

His leg stretches, thigh stretches, back stretches, neck.

The way he weaned himself from pain, the long addiction to silence, the years of aspirin and Valium and codeine and Darvon and scotch.

Bach. Monteverdi. Gesualdo. Palestrina. Sylvius Leopold Weiss.

The Ptolemaic measurement, the interlocking cones of memory, globe-girdling Poseidon. Waves.

Dean Fulbert, the sweet smell of cloves.

His lesson plans.

The dialectic, its beautiful logic and rigor, the numberless seraphim numbered and ranked, the orders of angels who heard when he cried and how he, counting, pinioned them.

The first sight he had of Catamount, the steep elm-girded entrance drive (diseased, gone, blighted now), the white frame houses spaced at equal intervals on the perimeter of Commons Lawn, the slate roofs glistening with snowmelt, the stone walls, lilacs, the whitewashed library, the beating of his heart.

Plato, Plotinus, Pythagoras, Pericles, Plato, Plotinus, Pythagoras, Pericles.

Beth.

Oh don't you remember the days of courting
When you'd lay your head upon my breast?
You could make me believe, by the falling of your arms,
That the sun rose in the West.

His daughter, unacknowledged.

His daughter, grown, not twenty miles away, a gift.

His health not what it ought to be, the way the headaches came at night, the fibrillation in his chest, the floaters when he shut his eyes.

The way she touched her tongue to his shut eyes now lingeringly.

The way midsummer turned to fall, then fall to early winter, then the New Year and the frozen months and the slow, what was the word? regeneration, redress?

His one true love restored.

All that fall and winter they shared the house in the orchard, on what Elizabeth called a second honeymoon and Paul averred could not properly be called their second, because they'd had no first. They postponed the trip to Italy, since Michael crated up her things and sent them to the address in Vermont. The morning light was bright, and she liked to watch the way the shadows of the trees inclined, shifting angles on the hillside, and the way they leaned towards the waiting house. She remembered how, long years before, he would climb out on the porch roof to dislodge the weight of what had fallen in the night. When the snow fell it fell heavily, and when she woke and watched the meadow or the orchard whitely blanketed she felt herself a child again, and desired to build snowmen and snow families or to inscribe snow angels on the hill.

Twice—once by invitation, once by accidental encounter—they shared a drink with Sam and Barbara Axelrod. These occasions were less dramatic than had been the first meeting, however, and by unspoken agreement the four maintained a kind of social distance. There seemed nothing useful to say. They could not pretend to intimacy or even to previous friendship, and the accident that joined them was no longer news.

Elizabeth began to know her daughter better and spoke to her often by phone. One afternoon in Rutland Sally met a lawyer from Washington, D.C. He had arrived in town on business, deposing a witness at the radio station where Sally worked; they had dinner together that evening and took in the nine o'clock showing of *Babe*. If you like pigs, she told her mother, it's a terrific movie, but I don't find them all that interesting, really. I liked *him*, though, I really did, he's cool. His name is Tim—Timothy—Albright, and he's thirty-two years old and used to play tennis at Yale. He was married once, but long ago, and he said he's tired of pretending to be happy "batching it" and wants to settle down. Oh I know what you're thinking, too good to be true, but it feels like he's the one.

The next day Sally accompanied her new friend to Burlington, where he deposed another witness, and they walked the shores of Lake Champlain and talked intensely for hours. They spent the following weekend at his apartment in Washington, in Cleveland Park, and by March they were engaged and planning to marry in June. It feels so *right*, Sally insisted, leaving her mother no room to maneuver, it feels just the way you say *you* felt, except that I'm not pregnant yet but yes we do want to have kids.

To Ballard these new complications were remarkable, astonishing, the world from which he'd held aloof now knocking on his door. Elizabeth was unsurprised; she had the habit of mothering—of talking, listening, advising—and she took Sally shopping and, once a week, the women met for lunch.

They discussed Sally's engagement, her long-standing interest in movies, her desire to have Sam not Paul be the father who gave her away at the altar, and whether that would be a problem in the ceremony and, once settled in D.C., her future plans. Elizabeth made herself useful: she said of course the Axelrods should be the ones who represent your family but of course we want to be there too, and someday soon I hope you'll meet Bill and Serena, I really want to bring them here and complete the circle. It's fascinating, isn't it, how what we used to call the nuclear family can—is this the right word?—metastasize, and six degrees of separation means everyone knows everyone; it's fascinating, isn't it, how sooner or later we meet . . .

But the deep fascination lay elsewhere. It lay in the house in the orchard, red flaking paint, ramshackle furniture, and in the bookshelves filled and tables piled high precariously with books, Paul standing there. The truth was when he smiled at her distraction fell away. The truth was how the rest of life was only the rest of her life.

"I wrote you all those letters."

"What?"

"Well, some of them I never sent. And some I wrote in my head only. Except you didn't answer . . ."

"You're sure you sent them? Letters?"

"Yes."

"To this address?"

Elizabeth regarded him. "Thus I refute Ballard," she said.

"Are you happy?"

"Yes. Is something wrong?"

"No."

"*Veramente*? Truthfully?"

"There's nothing wrong," he said.

"What's wrong?"

"I worry a little."

"About?"

"Oh, us, the two of us. If we deserve such happiness. If we will know how to maintain our good fortune. Preserve it."

"By counting our blessings," she said. "By not taking them for granted."

He shook his head.

"You're being superstitious, Paul. It isn't a question of 'fortune' or 'how to maintain it' or 'happiness' or 'maintenance' or anything abstract like that. We're not playing a zero-sum game, you and I; it's not as if we bank bad luck, or good luck, and get to invest it for the future . . ."

"You're young," he said. "Well, anyway, you're a lot younger than I am and you're still an optimist."

"What I am is grateful," she said.

He was sitting on the porch. He had not been feeling well. His head ached and his eyesight blurred and he could not complete the paragraph he started, so went outside to sit. On the armrest of the rocking chair, Ballard balanced a warm cup of tea. The cup was chipped, his favorite, the one with a pattern of ivy and a garland of blue flowers at the lip. He was rocking abstractedly, slowly, watching a sparrow and crow where the sparrow gained the greater height and dove and scoldingly drove back the black intruder from what must have been a nest. He was considering the question of whether or not a useful distinction might be drawn between those who think that, dying, the soul ascends to heaven and those who believe by contrast that heaven descends to collect the blessed soul—the argument, effectively, between the proposition that this lower world is immanent within the sphere above and the counter-proposition it stays separate, remembering that those who argue for disseverance assert the semi-permeable membrane of the spirit may not be sugared over, glossed, or presented—even metaphorically or (that *sine qua non* of all discourse concerning faith) in figurative speech—as a matter of osmosis or, alternatively, explained and justified by the doctrinal certainty of judgment, of foreordained damnation or salvation, insisting it is *not* here, it is *elsewhere*, it is *otherness*, whereas those who argue for a kind of continuity, that heaven might reside on earth, deploy instead the model or procedure of plasmolysis, and this was what he'd tried to say, a half a century before, to his school friend Robert Askeles (who went to law school and who married and had children and specialized in tax law and bought himself a condo in Zermatt)—now hearing Beth in the kitchen, running water, playing music, arranging lilies from the cutting garden back behind the peonies (their great heads drooping and their petals blown), the evening air foregathering above the hill, the faint hint of rain, was thinking how his life had come to have, what, *gravitas*? what, *harmony*? and how his lover brought him peace that passed not so much perhaps all understanding as description, for it was beyond his power, for it beggared definition, was raising the cup when the telephone rang and the sparrow, diving, sang, *Allerseelen, Alcuin*, although the sound was immanent, inside his head, and what he took for the ringing was silence, was shrill light, was nothing he knew how to hear.

Unaccountably Paul Ballard spilled his tea. He tried

to stand. He tried to stop rocking. He tried to cry out his love's name. And when she did come to the porch — *osmosis, plasmolysis* — still wearing her apron, her arms filled with flowers, it was as though — *gravitas, harmony* — Elizabeth was everywhere, was standing there above him where he fell. So what he did was rise and rise and where he was was at her strong right hand and this certainty and knowledge were a comfort to him in that final instant for she filled and was his vision. Ballard died.

XI

AND SO SHE was alone. Elizabeth stayed on without him. What came to pass had come to pass and there was nothing she could do or could have done; it was part of a pattern beyond her control. At every moment, faced with choice, she lived with the illusion that she in fact had *had* a choice and *had* a chance to alter what would happen or had happened or was happening. But she could not change it at all. By the time she reached him he was dead; by the time she called the ambulance, refusing to believe it, he was already stiffening; his tongue lolled out and his neck bent sideways at an impossible angle, his eyes rolling back in his head. The men brought a stretcher and blanket; they said "We're sorry, ma'am, it's hard, it always is, it don't look like he even knew . . ." and covered the body and left. She watched them load Paul Ballard in the van.

As a child she had believed in happy endings, or tried to, and when her own children were young she told them tales with happy endings—of frogs transformed to princes, and princesses set free from moatsurrounded towers or a century of sleep because of a kind kiss. Her children clamored for such fables, sitting on her lap or by the fireplace or lying in their beds, and Elizabeth invented freely what she could not quite remember. The ferocious lion would recognize his benefactor, Androcles, and by offering an outstretched paw refrain from mortal combat; the wicked witch would be outwitted by a songbird or a dwarf.

In her telling, always, the third son solved a riddle although other members of his family made fun of him, or the fire-breathing dragon was transmogrified to gentle steed or the humble cottage was revealed to be a castle. Always virtue triumphed over evil while good fairies waved their magic wands, and everything that had seemed lost was, on the instant, restored. Straw turned to gold and chaff to wheat and water into wine.

So there must have been another way her story could conclude, a turning on the forest path that led not into darker wood but a sun-dappled glade. Her children expected such satisfaction, always; always they would chorus, "Mommy, tell us *that* one, tell it to us again." The enchanted prince would waken when his faithful milkmaid kissed him, and would prove a perfect chevalier although in outward aspect, sleeping, he had seemed but a brute beast. He would ascend his kingdom's throne and make the milkmaid queen. Then the lovers would embrace and, amid general rejoicing and much public celebration, wed. Everybody would go to the seashore and live happily ever after, and their delight would prove eternal and there would be no sorrow and nothing to grieve for, no grief.

Therefore Elizabeth did try to change this final chapter, and lying in her bed at night dreamed other versions of their story. It deserved a happy ending, she was sure. Tossing and wakeful, unable to sleep, she imagined Paul Ballard alive. Night after night, with no children to talk to and no fire crackling in the hearth, she revised their history. Though she had taken a wrong turning and he too had blundered from the path they would hear each other's heartfelt cries and be reunited; tall aspens and the evergreens and bramble-tangled hawthorn would part to light their way. In a leafy bower they would meet and kiss and lie down on a bed of boughs and wake up in each other's arms, transformed. Old flesh would fall away like scales; the very scales upon his eyes—mild cataracts, myopia—would shuck off like shed skin.

Instead what she saw was him slumped in the rocking chair, then on the floor. The floor required paint. The rocker's middle spindle had at some point come unglued. The rocker's cane seat needed mending; she would see to it next fall. When Ballard crumpled as he fell he did so with precision: the right arm raised, then the left leg extended, and then the whole body contracting. In bed at night she pictured this as a balletic movement, a supple and a practiced gesture intended to instruct. But instead what she saw when she rushed to his side was the way his mouth jerked open and his cheeks went into spasm and his tongue hung out. She had the impression he wanted to speak, had had something he needed to say. Yet she could hear nothing coherent, only the murmurous gargle of air, only the sound of her own shouted "No!"

To a stranger, she remembered thinking afterwards, all this would appear, if not melodramatic, dramatic; to someone watching from the street it might even seem rehearsed. It must have looked astonishing: an old man falling to the floor, a woman reaching out for him as though for an embrace. But no one watched them from the street and there was nothing to see.

She could not remember how long she had cradled him or how long she waited—one minute, three minutes, ten, fifteen?—before running to the kitchen and dialing 911. His neck was rigid and his pupils were dilated and later she learned these were all standard symptoms; visibly Paul Ballard stiffened while audibly she wept. She should not blame herself, they said, or the emergency medical team; it could not have been prevented no matter how they tried.

Nonetheless, she tried. She imagined Paul Ballard alive. They would begin again, Elizabeth imagined, and he would not be ill or frail, and they would rock together on the front-porch rocker of a house equivalent to this one, in a village not an orchard, set back from Main Street, and watch the parade—men with flutes and horns, men playing drums and trumpets, and then the smiling high-stepping baton twirlers and drum majorettes—pass by. They would wave at friends and relatives, and girls on horseback would prance near the curb, and the Kiwanis Club would march

down Main Street also, displaying their peculiar rib-
bons and their particular caps. The sky would be the
halcyon blue of spring, of possibility, and flags would
wave in a light breeze and birds would warble sweetly
while she took her lover's hand. She and Paul would
stroll the marble paving of North Catamount each
morning, rain or shine.

But the truth of it was otherwise; the truth is she had
known for years that hers was a story of failure, not
success. She was forty-eight years old, and neither divorced nor a widow, yet everything that mattered lay
behind her, not ahead. They would enjoy no quiet retirement, no "best is yet to be" or silver threads among
the gold or Memorial Day or Independence Day parade on Main Street while they rocked and watched.
Elizabeth knew she was being romantic, and being
sentimental, but such knowledge made no difference
and she could not console herself or avoid self-pity and
the sense of failed romance. What she wanted was not
hers to have; what she had she did not want.

At other times she asked herself how things might
have been different, how his illness could have been diagnosed or have followed a different course. Preven-
tive medicine, she knew, was all the rage these days;
there might have been a remedy if they had acted earlier; there might have been an operation or a treatment
consisting of drugs. The doctors could have warned
her what was happening, or what would happen if he
did not have a bypass or angioplasty or some experi-
mental yet low-risk procedure; they could have pre-
scribed blood-thinners or anticoagulants or changed

his diet radically or done reconstructive surgery or whatever it is that they do nowadays to alter the way the body works and repair a damaged artery or replace a neural pathway in the brain. In this manner they would have avoided what the doctors called a massive insult to his system, and by which they themselves were insulted, since it called their own professional competence into question. He had had, they assured her, an inoperable berry aneurysm and weakness they could not detect.

She herself remained as healthy as a horse. It seemed a strange expression, since horses can be sickly too, and susceptible to injury or unexplained collapse. But Elizabeth had taken her own health for granted, always, and did not know what "angioplasty" or "anti-coagulant" or "neural pathway" really meant, and what she remembered from high school failed to supply a useful or important distinction between a damaged artery and a ruptured vein. She did not know the options or the success rate of operations or the likelihood of failure or the method of detection in a CAT scan or MRI or EKG or all those machines and diagnostic procedures with initials that were supposed to comfort you and convince you of the excellence of modern medicine. Was the cerebral aneurysm an insult to the heart or brain, she wondered, and how could such an insult be prevented from leading on to injury? What would have been the options if the stroke had been less massive and the cerebral rupture less complete? He did not have to die. He might have lived.

Around her, life continued; daily there was mail delivered—bills and circulars and promotional offers for cereal and credit cards and a surprising number of condolence notes and letters—and there were telephone calls. People made and kept and broke appointments and the radio made noise when she turned it on, as did the TV. There were local elections and national elections and wars and peace treaties and airline disasters and famine and floods. His death, so unexpected, meant she needed to attend to things: the disposition of the body, the newspaper announcement, the question of survivors and, since there were no other survivors, the will. There were financial statements to receive and doctors' bills to pay. There were bankers and real estate assessors and probate lawyers to meet, for it transpired he had left her everything, and the house and land had value, as did his pictures and books.

Bill and Serena flew to Albany, and she collected them and drove them to North Catamount and was, for a weekend, occupied. They exclaimed about the view, the orchard, and they approved of her decision to remain in Vermont, at least for a few weeks or months until things settled down. Her children said, We're here for you, we want to make it better and we want to help. But they had never known Paul Ballard, and they did not know how to console her, or what to say and do. They radiated health and ignorance and the deep self-absorption of youth. She showed them her old college, and the points of local interest and, when Monday morning came, she returned them to the airport and to their separate planes. Serena said, "We hate to leave," and she said, "Yes, I hate to see you go," and Bill said, "We'll be back, Mom, we promise, we'll come back soon," and they kissed and parted quickly, with relief.

Sally's marriage to Timothy Albright at the end of June took place without Elizabeth. She and Paul had planned to join the ceremony, but when the time arrived she could not bring herself to leave the house or drive to Sandgate alone. The wedding was held at the Axelrod home and presided over by a justice of the peace. The young couple desired no religious service, no formal gowns or wedding march, since Tim had been married before, but there would be music and dancing and dinner underneath a tent. The two of them wrote their own vows. They memorized Shakespeare's sonnet, the one that begins, "Let me not to the marriage of true minds admit impediments," and planned to recite it in unison and change the final phrase to "nor no one ever loved," because it would be exclusionary to say "nor no *man* ever loved." Then each of them composed a speech about what they were hoping for in marriage, and confidently expecting, and how they were willing to work hard at it and grateful for the chance. Sally showed her mother her own first avowal, and its revisions—she was keeping the speech a secret from Tim, as he was keeping his from her— and they discussed what would and would not be appropriate to say. "I really, really hope I don't choke up," said Sally, and Elizabeth assured her "You'll be perfect, you'll be fine."

Elizabeth too wrote a speech. She was planning to thank Sam and Barbara Axelrod for making her so welcome, for letting Paul and her join in the celebration; she felt as though this last year she had recovered what was lost and had found a buried treasure, a few of the guests here will know what I mean, and she wished the happy couple years and, given the time frame, *centuries* of happiness. In the coming century, she hoped, they would be just as blissful together as in this. She purchased a new dress in a Manchester boutique: of gray silk, ankle-length, with a cowl neckline and white appliqué roses on the sleeves, and she prepared herself to recognize and be able to identify the guest list: which of her daughter's friends came from college, which from work, which of the families attending were Axelrod family friends. She and Paul conferred at length as to their wedding gift, and what would be appropriate: two tickets to Italy, money, a car, or the Grandma Moses rooster their daughter professed to admire. They settled on this last.

Then Ballard died and was cremated, and she could not bear to attend. When Sally called, the day before, Elizabeth excused herself: I'd be useless, she said, I'd be worse than useless and please go ahead without me, please, I'll be thinking about you all day. Oh Mother, said Sally, but Elizabeth was adamant: I'd make a scene, she said, I'd make a weepy spectacle. You understand, said Sally, I can't cancel or postpone it, and her mother said, of course I understand, of course you can't postpone.

On the morning of the wedding, she took the urn with Ballard's ashes from the high shelf in the pantry where she'd stored it since his cremation and, with his sharp-edged shovel and a paper bag of grass seed, walked out into the orchard on the west side of the house. It was going to be a hot day. Already the meadow beyond the vegetable garden shimmered, and bees were at the apple blossoms and mosquitoes at her ear. She hoped it would not thunder later on. Consciously, she wondered if the weather up in Sandgate would be similar or if the range of intervening hills might change the weather pattern, so that the stormy weather here might be, one valley over, clear. The urn felt weightless, incorporeal, and she had wavered all that week as to whether to unseal the cap and spread the ashes or to bury them within their container; when the time arrived, she promised herself, she would choose.

A plane broke what she heard as silence, traversing Glastenbury Mountain. She was not wearing gloves. In an act she recognized even while performing it as needless and premonitory, a ritual solicitude, Elizabeth balanced the urn upright six paces from the spot she had selected earlier and, when it again threatened to topple, leaned his ashes up against the base of an apple tree trunk.

Then she commenced to dig. The ground was hard, resistant, and her shovel severed roots. After four or five such shovelfuls, a splinter lodged in her right palm and she felt astonished by and then grateful for the pain. She bit her palm and pulled the splinter out between her teeth, licking and sucking the few drops of blood. Within sight of the kitchen, she dug a hole beneath the apple tree and—unable to look at his ashes, the bits of granulated bone—buried the urn in the space she had fashioned, then tamped it over carefully.

Next she spread grass seed on top. The bag of seed had been in Ballard's potting shed, and she had no way of knowing if it was new, or old, still germinant, and this made her indecisive as to how much grass was needed, so she kept adding seed to the small bare created patch beneath her feet. Then, finally, with a gesture that signaled completion, she tore the paper end to end and emptied everything out.

In September she did try to leave, and flew to Detroit, then Marquette. Once more Elizabeth rented a car—this time a dark blue Mercury—and drove to the shores of Lake Huron, then the camp in Hessel. Bill joined her in Marquette. He was returning to college, but he had been part of the work crew and wanted to show her what he had accomplished: the work of repair was complete. Over the previous summer, construction had proceeded and the shingle roof had been replaced, together with those picture windows firemen had had to break in order to gain entry.

Bill pointed out details with pride. There was a new front door, and dining nook, and the outdoor shower had been improved. The wood had not been painted yet, since they wanted her to choose the color for the shutters and the window trim, but the lake-facing deck had been enlarged. "I built this, Mom," he told her. "I countersunk that sucker, we drove this piling six feet down. Me and the guys . . ."

The day was overcast, and she could not see Drummond Island or locate the nearby and low-flying loons; fish surfaced at intervals, jumping, and a man in a skiff idled past. A pile of wood scraps for burning had been mounded by the barbecue, and there were tire tracks everywhere.

"I love it here," said Bill.

"Yes."

"I love what it feels like to sit on this deck."

"I know you do. I used to, too."

"I spoke to Dad," he said. "He sends his best. He hopes you're okay."

"I am," she said.

"You are?"

"When you speak to him the next time tell him everything is hunky-dory. Tip-top. What are he and Giovanni up to these days?"

"Up to?"

Elizabeth nodded.

"Dad's painting the downstairs hallway—making a mural, he says. Of centaurs, is it, satyrs?—half-man, half-horse. You know."

"Oh yes," she said. "The mythical beasts with their

lyres and spears. The maidens with bunches of grapes."

"Whatever."

"I don't think this will work," she said. "Not for me, I mean, not today. It's wonderful, darling, the way you took this project over, the way that you improved the house, and I'm proud of what you've learned and everything you've done."

"But?"

"Where I belong is Vermont. I don't expect you to believe me or to understand, but I feel if I *wait* there, if I just stay there alone and intensely enough I'll make some sense of everything. It isn't very grown-up, maybe, and it isn't, oh, *sensible*, but I can't help feeling Paul Ballard wants me to stay. There's a message he's sending, *transmitting*, and I need to be in Catamount in order to receive it . . ."

Bill sat. It embarrassed him, she knew, to hear her talk like this. He did not want to think his mother could be so nakedly in need of comfort and support; she was supposed to be a parent not a child.

"The point is there's this thing that happened to me, really *happened* to me, darling, and I can't pretend it didn't, can't just turn my back and leave . . ."

"Whatever," he repeated, running his hand along the guardrail of the deck he'd built.

"It's not superstition," she told him. "It's what feels right to me now."

They spent the night in Hessell. Bill built a fire out of the construction scraps, and they grilled sausages and steak and consumed potatoes and corn and a bottle of wine. Over coffee they discussed what courses he was planning to take, and at midnight he rolled out his sleeping bag while she lay in her old room and tried to fall asleep. But a vision of the future—herself old in the new century, desolation, desolation—appeared each time she shut her eyes, and therefore Elizabeth sat up and read. She read *A Treasury of the World's Great Love Letters* and *Anne of Green Gables* and *Songs the Whalemen Sang*. Moths battered at the bedroom light, and hurtled at the screens. In the morning there was bright easterly light, and the lake stretched out before her like an invitation, but she turned her back on it and drove to the airport and said to her son, "I'm sorry, I'm so sorry, but maybe I'll be better company next summer. Maybe we could try again." And then she flew to Albany and pulled into the driveway of the house that was her only home while he flew on to Raleigh-Durham and his junior year at Duke.

"Elizabeth?"

"Yes?"

"There you are. It's Barbara. Barbara Axelrod."

"Hello."

"I've been calling and calling. It's been, oh, ages since we saw each other. And we missed you at the wedding. We so were hoping you would come."

"I wanted to," she said.

"It's hard, I know. It must be hard."

She held the receiver. She waited.

"Hello? Hello?"

"I hear you."

"I'm using the car phone, that's why. I'm on the way to Price Chopper, the one in Manchester. Your voice is fading in and out."

"Why are you calling, Barbara?"

"I wanted to drive down for you. I wanted to send someone, anyone, to bring you to the wedding. It was beautiful."

"I'm sure it was."

"And now there are the photographs, Sally ordered you a set. We have them now, they just arrived, and it's amazing, isn't it, how the first time we all met it was also because of a wedding. When was that, only, what was it, fifteen months ago?"

"Sixteen."

"Amazing how much has been happening since. How much has changed, I mean, now she's moved down to Washington."

"And Paul is dead."

"Oh yes, I meant that too. We wanted to ask you to dinner tonight, or tomorrow, if you're busy, which is why I'm buying out, oh, everything in Price Chopper. They're here for the weekend . . ."

"Who?"

"Sally and Tim. Do come."

"It's kind of you. And Sam," she said. "And Sally too, of course. And Tim. But no."

In the kitchen she made tea. While the tea leaves steeped she put his breadboard and his garlic press and bread knife and his spatula away. She took his teacup from the rack, the one that he was drinking from the day he died, and threw it at the floor and watched it break. It was heavy and well made and did not come apart or shatter easily; the handle fell off but the bowl stayed intact, and so she had to pick it up again and throw it at the wall before the body of the cup exploded. She ran cold water over her hands, attempting to calm herself, trying to stop. Then with a rush of anger she threw the stool he liked to sit on hard against the corner cupboard, and the glass shivered and broke.

For all that afternoon, and the night to follow and in the morning, when she woke, Elizabeth could not forgive him. They had spent too little time together for it to be over already; Paul Ballard had left things behind, and it enraged Elizabeth to be one of the things he had left. Why hadn't he reached out to her from his hospital bed or during the period of recuperation or for all those long years afterwards while she drifted and hovered and waited, expecting his call? What could he have been dreaming of that did not include her, and for what possible reason did he will her this house to attend to? Why had he shackled her, like a grim ghost, to their shared past: the rocking chair abandoned, the floor where he fell needing paint . . .

She asked herself these questions all the more insistently because he could not answer them, and did not while alive. Elizabeth felt cheated of the future and cheated of the present, and she came to feel that his behavior had been cowardly as well as inattentive. It was as though, instead of arguing, he simply disappeared; instead of practicing what he had preached—the joys of disputation, the value of debate—he slammed the door and left. He had been, in his carelessness, cruel.

Over time she came to blame herself for having proved so gullible, for having reveled in—there was no other way to describe it—the operatic gestures of romance. She had been—there was no other word for it—abandoned. Years before she'd seen a movie called *Seduced and Abandoned*, a creaky little Italian comedy that she could barely remember. No doubt it starred Marcello Mastroianni or some moustache-twirling dandy out of central casting; no doubt it ended well. It had provided an excuse for some young beauty to be photographed, and scenery, and local color shoveled on in shovelfuls. The girl had or hadn't become pregnant, and she did or didn't get the guy, and did or didn't continue in the movies, and probably in actual life she slept with the producer or had a nervous breakdown or ruined her career with drugs, and probably the whole thing had been shot on the cheap in Cinecittà or the streets of Positano. There may have been romantic complications and a theme song with accordions or a hurdy-gurdy; Elizabeth could not be sure; it was all too vague, too long ago. But she did remember the title, *Seduced and Abandoned*, and it was the phrase in her head.

So she compiled a grievance list: the way he had not followed her to Grosse Pointe Shores, or known about her pregnancy, or understood how much he failed to understand. He might note and come to write about the sonorous distinction between mass and Mass, between Massenet and Masséna, the connotations of intonation in colloquial discourse and the usage of orthography as a pattern for set speech; he might trace and disentangle the tangled skein of lineage that reduced poor Jason Newcomb to a wheelchair and a smiling lunacy, might define that fleeting moment during the Blitzkrieg in London when English people saw themselves as classless, not class-ridden, or at least believed themselves to be a single populace in a single shared predicament, and describe this myth of solidarity as a legacy of siege, more similar in spirit to Periclean Athens than was London pride before or since—might write his articles and books with no concern as to their audience, since what Ballard had delighted in was private not public interpretation, the cabinet of curiosities, the taxonomy of wonder, and looking up at last from his pad of yellow foolscap or his typewriter would blink at her and wipe his eyes and ask, what time is it, what have you been doing, Beth, what should we do about dinner?

She made no answer. She poured herself a cup of tea and drew the kitchen curtains and turned off the light. She dropped wine glasses and his coffee mugs and flower-trimmed blue plates and accumulated fragments of pottery and broken glass on the tile floor. She would sweep it up tomorrow, or maybe the day after that.

She still could leave North Catamount. She did not need to stay. Some other women might have known Paul Ballard was a poor sort of risk, no bargain, or have understood much sooner that the news he was was bad. Some other women would have tried to eradicate his memory, to close the book and call it quits and leave well enough alone. But she had been seduced, then abandoned, and there was nowhere else to go and nothing else to do. Elizabeth could not erase the image of his hand on hers, the burning dottle of his pipe, the hats he wore in stormy weather and the way he worked his mouth in sleep, the angle of his right foot where he walked. She tried to and could not renounce the dialectic he had taught, the way he introduced their class to Plato, Aquinas, Hobbes and Locke, the love of learning he conveyed, the declamatory presence of his body in the room. In their shared syntax all was apposite, subordinate, the conjunction of his arms with hers and interrogatory of his eyebrows, the antithetical construction of his shadow on the lamplit wall and the fierce imperative of his upright cock. In her memory it all came together, all jumbled, not only object and subject but also noun and verb: despair, to despair, love, to love.

"Are you waiting?"

"Yes."

"Where?"

"Here. I'm here, my darling."

"Can you hear me?"

"Yes. Completely."

"Clearly?"

"Oh so clearly, Paul. Can't you hear me hearing you? Where are you?"

"Where?"

"In the kitchen?"

"The kitchen. The living room."

"Where? Where?"

"Here on the porch."

"It doesn't matter."

"Everywhere."

"Can you see me?"

"No. Not now."

"Can't you see me?"

"No."

Thereafter Elizabeth stayed in the house, playing a role of some importance in local politics, deeding her property to the Land Conservation Program and giving money to the library and schools. When the Holbein Memorial Hospital built a nursing-care facility on the west edge of the village, she funded the design of flowerbeds and paid for the planting and benches, and once a week she volunteered to read to patients on the oncology ward. She joined the Catamount Garden Club and served as a vice-president of the Vermont chapter of Planned Parenthood and the ACLU. In small ways Elizabeth helped the college also, donating Paul Ballard's books and papers, with the exception of his letters, those he had not finished or had failed to send; she funded a scholarship in Ballard's name. Successive presidents of Catamount College approached her for a major gift in order to endow a wing of the new library, and she declined.

She left his shirts and pants and jackets hanging in the closet, and she kept the door of the closet shut so the smell would not fade or diminish; she retained Ballard's toothbrush and his hairbrush in the bathroom, with his hair nestled in the bristles, and the half-empty bottle of Old Spice, his cheap cologne. She stored his notebooks and his shoes and the book he had been reading, with the page turned down where he had left it when he ceased to read. The solitude that others urged her to avoid was healing, balm in Gilead, and he was always at her side although she seemed alone. Because he occupied the house she was not lonely inside it, and because he kept her company she did not feel afraid.

She saw her children often. Sally and Tim, as they had promised in their marriage ceremony, admitted no impediments; his law career prospered and after he made partner they discovered a mutual interest in golf. Within a year of their wedding Sally announced she was pregnant, and soon enough Elizabeth became the grandmother of someone called Roger Bernard Axelrod-Sieverdsen Albright, who seemed too insubstantial to carry that name and whom she called Jolly Roger, because he smiled and clapped his hands and cackled happily the instant she appeared. When their second child was two years old, the Albrights moved from Cleveland Park to Bethesda; the school system would be better there, Sally declared, and she wanted to be able to let Roger and Corinne play outside without having to worry or feel she had to supervise them in the yard all day.

Serena, too, would marry, though her choice was less successful and, after two years, on the grounds of incompatibility, she and her husband divorced. By this time she was working as a curator at the Smithsonian, in the furniture department, and she came home one evening to discover he had spray-painted the sideboard and poured paint remover on the finish of the tea table in the living room and packed up his own things and left. "I hate it, Mom, I *hate* it," she said, "it's like I've been so *stupid*, like I was in a nightmare or sleepwalking or something. Did you feel that way, did you ever?" and she answered "Yes."

William stayed quiet, self-possessed, and—although he remained very handsome, a blend of her lean angularity and his father's dark insouciance—alone. It took her longer than it should have, Elizabeth knew, to recognize that he preferred his animals to the company of people and that he was happy carving antlers into coat racks and lamp bases and ashtrays, and selling them at

Upper Peninsula craft fairs and in local curio shoppes. He winterized the camp in Hessel and moved there with his dogs, a pair of Gordon setters; he sent her monthly handwritten painstaking letters about the weather and fish. He wrote that she should consider a dog as a replacement for Ecco, and he promised he would breed and train a Gordon setter for her, and described in detail the behavior of his dogs.

She did meet Michael Vire again, when he lay dying in the hospital in Baltimore. In Italy the doctors had been first optimistic, then grave, then in disagreement, and therefore Michael flew to America—as he and she had done together many years before, when they had feared their daughter might go deaf. Serena arranged a meeting with her assistant's husband, who was a surgeon at Johns Hopkins, but by the time he was admitted to the hospital the cancer had spread from the liver and was everywhere, inoperable, and he asked Elizabeth if she would come on down to say goodbye. She said, "Of course I can, of course I will," and stayed with Sally in Bethesda, visiting the grandchildren; she had to steel herself to see him, but it proved surprisingly easy and he was surprisingly brave. He was gray and thin and bald and bent, but he retained his offhand charm; this business of dying, Michael declared, has been overrated. When she asked him if he felt much pain, he said, "It doesn't hurt as much as I'd always expected it would, it's only that I need it to be over soon, *passata la festa.*"

"What was the other part?" she asked, and he seemed pleased that she could not remember. "*Finita la commedia*," said Michael, and gave a little hiccough-laugh and, lying back in the hospital bed, appeared to fall asleep. She took a taxi to Sally's, where Roger and Corinne were having their dinner and watching TV. They said, "It's pizza, Granny," waving, not taking their eyes off the screen.

She said, "Hello, my darlings," and poured herself a glass of cold white wine. There, sitting in the TV room, quietly, while Bugs Bunny jumped from cliff to cliff and a family called Flintstone read tablet-books and played with their pet dinosaurs, remembering the quick and dead, she wept. "What's the matter, Granny?" Roger asked, and she said, "Nothing, darling, only something in my eye."

Elizabeth returned to North Catamount next day. It had snowed the night before, and Tommy Epps had not been by to plow, so the white expanse of lawn and driveway and orchard remained intact; snow drifted on the porch stairs. From the furnace chimney came a plume of smoke, and she watched it rise and dissipate. She let herself into the house. There, entering, she understood—by the stale smell of the unaired rooms, the bare refrigerator and the sudden shocking image of herself in the hall mirror—that she was growing old. She folded the shutters and opened the windows and in order to maintain the heat turned up the thermostat; she did not care, not care.

There are few men and women who have what can fairly be called a great passion, and she was one of those few. She had shared her youth and middle age with someone she adored and who adored her equally.

She had been, she told herself, blessed. The love had transfigured them each and both; the record of their devotion was hers to remember and keep. He, too, was fortunate in this: she gave him, tongueless, voice. In her last years she wrote it down, and these are the lines that Elizabeth wrote. *I shall end a lengthy letter with a brief conclusion. Farewell, my only love.*